Favorite
Father Brown Stories

G. K. CHESTERTON

DOVER PUBLICATIONS, INC.
New York

DOVER THRIFT EDITIONS

GENERAL EDITOR: STANLEY APPELBAUM
EDITOR OF THIS VOLUME: PHILIP SMITH

Published in Canada by General Publishing Company, Ltd.,
30 Lesmill Road, Don Mills, Toronto, Ontario.
Published in the United Kingdom by Constable and Company, Ltd.,
3 The Lanchesters, 162–164 Fulham Palace Road, London W6 9ER.

This Dover edition, first published in 1993,
is an original selection of stories from
The Innocence of Father Brown (Cassell & Co., Ltd., London, 1911)
and *The Wisdom of Father Brown* (Cassell & Co., Ltd., London, 1914).
The selection was made by John Grafton, who also
wrote the new introductory Note.

Manufactured in the United States of America
Dover Publications, Inc.
31 East 2nd Street
Mineola, N.Y. 11501

Library of Congress Cataloging-in-Publication Data

Chesterton, G. K. (Gilbert Keith), 1874–1936.
Favorite Father Brown stories / G. K. Chesterton.
p.   cm. — (Dover thrift editions)
ISBN 0-486-27545-0
1. Brown, Father (Fictitious character)—Fiction.   2. Detective
and mystery stories, English.   I. Title.   II. Series.
PR4453.C4A6   1993
823′.912—dc20   92–36570
CIP

Note

GILBERT KEITH CHESTERTON was born in London on May 29, 1874, and before the turn of the century established himself as a free-lance journalist and reviewer. From the publication in 1900 of his first book of poetry, *The Wild Knight*, until his death in 1936, Chesterton was one of the most prolific and best-known figures on the English literary scene. During those three and a half decades he turned out dozens of volumes of political and social commentary, literary criticism and biography, theological essays, poetry, short stories and novels. Among his best-known works of fiction are *The Napoleon of Notting Hill* (1904) and *The Man Who Was Thursday* (1908).

To the connoisseur of the detective short story in its classic form, the five volumes that chronicle the adventures of Chesterton's priest-detective Father Brown are unique in the genre. The Father Brown stories comprise one of the few sequences that may be compared, for inventiveness and charm, with the work of Chesterton's great contemporary Arthur Conan Doyle. The six stories in this collection, from the first two Father Brown books, *The Innocence of Father Brown* (1911) and *The Wisdom of Father Brown* (1914), trace the sleuth's early adventures, which often feature the arch-criminal Flambeau (who after a brief spell as Brown's adversary retires from his life of crime to become the cleric's friend and frequent companion). The later volumes were *The Incredulity of Father Brown* (1926), *The Secret of Father Brown* (1927) and *The Scandal of Father Brown* (1935).

Contents

The Blue Cross

BETWEEN THE SILVER ribbon of morning and the green glittering ribbon of sea, the boat touched Harwich and let loose a swarm of folk like flies, among whom the man we must follow was by no means conspicuous—nor wished to be. There was nothing notable about him, except a slight contrast between the holiday gaiety of his clothes and the official gravity of his face. His clothes included a slight, pale grey jacket, a white waistcoat, and a silver straw hat with a grey-blue ribbon. His lean face was dark by contrast, and ended in a curt black beard that looked Spanish and suggested an Elizabethan ruff. He was smoking a cigarette with the seriousness of an idler. There was nothing about him to indicate the fact that the grey jacket covered a loaded revolver, that the white waistcoat covered a police card, or that the straw hat covered one of the most powerful intellects in Europe. For this was Valentin himself, the head of the Paris police and the most famous investigator of the world; and he was coming from Brussels to London to make the greatest arrest of the century.

Flambeau was in England. The police of three countries had tracked the great criminal at last from Ghent to Brussels, from Brussels to the Hook of Holland; and it was conjectured that he would take some advantage of the unfamiliarity and confusion of the Eucharistic Congress, then taking place in London. Probably he would travel as some minor clerk or secretary connected with it; but, of course, Valentin could not be certain; nobody could be certain about Flambeau.

It is many years now since this colossus of crime suddenly ceased keeping the world in a turmoil; and when he ceased, as they said after the death of Roland, there was a great quiet upon the earth. But in his best days (I mean, of course, his worst) Flambeau was a figure as statuesque and international as the Kaiser. Almost every morning the daily paper announced that he had escaped the consequences of one extraordinary

1

crime by committing another. He was a Gascon of gigantic stature and bodily daring; and the wildest tales were told of his outbursts of athletic humour; how he turned the *juge d'instruction* upside down and stood him on his head, "to clear his mind"; how he ran down the Rue de Rivoli with a policeman under each arm. It is due to him to say that his fantastic physical strength was generally employed in such bloodless though undignified scenes; his real crimes were chiefly those of ingenious and wholesale robbery. But each of his thefts was almost a new sin, and would make a story by itself. It was he who ran the great Tyrolean Dairy Company in London, with no dairies, no cows, no carts, no milk, but with some thousand subscribers. These he served by the simple operation of moving the little milk-cans outside people's doors to the doors of his own customers. It was he who had kept up an unaccountable and close correspondence with a young lady whose whole letter-bag was intercepted, by the extraordinary trick of photographing his messages infinitesimally small upon the slides of a microscope. A sweeping simplicity, however, marked many of his experiments. It is said he once repainted all the numbers in a street in the dead of night merely to divert one traveller into a trap. It is quite certain that he invented a portable pillar-box, which he put up at corners in quiet suburbs on the chance of strangers dropping postal orders into it. Lastly he was known to be a startling acrobat; despite his huge figure, he could leap like a grasshopper and melt into the treetops like a monkey. Hence the great Valentin, when he set out to find Flambeau, was perfectly well aware that his adventures would not end when he had found him.

But how was he to find him? On this the great Valentin's ideas were still in process of settlement.

There was one thing which Flambeau, with all his dexterity of disguise, could not cover, and that was his singular height. If Valentin's quick eye had caught a tall apple-woman, a tall grenadier, or even a tolerably tall duchess, he might have arrested them on the spot. But all along his train there was nobody that could be a disguised Flambeau, any more than a cat could be a disguised giraffe. About the people on the boat he had already satisfied himself; and the people picked up at Harwich or on the journey limited themselves with certainty to six. There was a short railway official travelling up to the terminus, three fairly short market-gardeners picked up two stations afterwards, one very short widow lady going up from a small Essex town, and a very short Roman Catholic priest going up from a small Essex village. When it came to the last case, Valentin gave it up and almost laughed. The little priest was so much the essence of those Eastern flats: he had a face as round and dull as a Norfolk dumpling; he had eyes as empty as the North Sea; he had several brown-paper parcels which he was quite incapable of collecting. The Eucharistic Congress had doubtless sucked out of their local stagnation many such creatures, blind and helpless, like moles disinterred. Valentin was a sceptic in the severe style of France, and could have no love for priests. But he could have pity for them, and this one might have provoked pity in anybody. He had a large, shabby umbrella, which constantly fell on the floor. He did not seem to know which was the right end of his return ticket. He explained with a moon-calf simplicity to everybody in the carriage that he had to be careful, because he had something made of real silver "with blue stones" in one of his brown-paper parcels. His quaint blending of Essex flatness with saintly simplicity continuously amused the Frenchman till the priest arrived (somehow) at Stratford with all his parcels, and came back for his umbrella. When he did the last, Valentin even had the good nature to warn him not to take care of the silver by telling everybody about it. But to whomever he talked, Valentin kept his eye open for someone else; he looked out steadily for anyone, rich or poor, male or female, who was well up to six feet; for Flambeau was four inches above it.

He alighted at Liverpool Street, however, quite conscientiously secure that he had not missed the criminal so far. He then went to Scotland Yard to regularize his position and arrange for help in case of need; he then lit another cigarette and went for a long stroll in the streets of London. As he was walking in the streets and squares beyond Victoria, he paused suddenly and stood. It was a quaint, quiet square, very typical of London, full of an accidental stillness. The tall, flat houses round looked at once prosperous and uninhabited; the square of shrubbery in the centre looked as deserted as a green Pacific islet. One of the four sides was much higher than the rest, like a dais; and the line of this side was broken by one of London's admirable accidents—a restaurant that looked as if it had strayed from Soho. It was an unreasonably attractive object, with dwarf plants in pots and long, striped blinds of lemon yellow and white. It stood specially high above the street, and in the usual patchwork way of London, a flight of steps from the street ran up to meet the front door almost as a fire-escape might run up to a first-floor window. Valentin stood and smoked in front of the yellow-white blinds and considered them long.

The most incredible thing about miracles is that they happen. A few clouds in heaven do come together into the staring shape of one human eye. A tree does stand up in the landscape of a doubtful journey in the exact and elaborate shape of a note of interrogation. I have seen both these things myself within the last few days. Nelson does die in the instant of victory; and a man named Williams does quite accidentally murder a man named Williamson; it sounds like a sort of infanticide. In short, there is in life an element of elfin coincidence which people reckoning on the prosaic may perpetually miss. As it has been well expressed in the paradox of Poe, wisdom should reckon on the unforeseen.

Aristide Valentin was unfathomably French; and the French intelligence is intelligence specially and solely. He was not "a thinking machine"; for that is a brainless phrase of modern fatalism and materialism. A machine only *is* a machine because it cannot think. But he was a thinking man, and a plain man at the same time. All his wonderful successes, that looked like conjuring, had been gained by plodding logic, by clear and commonplace French thought. The French electrify the world not by starting any paradox, they electrify it by carrying out a truism. They carry a truism so far—as in the French Revolution. But exactly because Valentin understood reason, he understood the limits of reason. Only a man who knows nothing of motors talks of motoring without petrol; only a man who knows nothing of reason talks of reasoning without strong, undisputed first principles. Here he had no strong first principles. Flambeau had been missed at Harwich; and if he was in London at all, he might be anything from a tall tramp on Wimbledon Common to a tall toastmaster at the Hôtel Métropole. In such a naked state of nescience, Valentin had a view and a method of his own.

In such cases he reckoned on the unforeseen. In such cases, when he could not follow the train of the reasonable, he coldly and carefully followed the train of the unreasonable. Instead of going to the right places—banks, police-stations, rendezvous—he systematically went to the wrong places; knocked at every empty house, turned down every *cul de sac*, went up every lane blocked with rubbish, went round every crescent that led him uselessly out of the way. He defended this crazy course quite logically. He said that if one had a clue this was the worst way; but if one had no clue at all it was the best, because there was just the chance that any oddity that caught the eye of the pursuer might be the same that had caught the eye of the pursued. Somewhere a man must begin, and it had better be just where another man might stop. Something about that flight of steps up to the shop, something about the quietude and quaintness of the restaurant, roused all the detective's rare romantic fancy and made him resolve to strike at random. He went up the steps, and sitting down by the window, asked for a cup of black coffee.

It was half-way through the morning, and he had not breakfasted; the slight litter of other breakfasts stood about on the table to remind him of his hunger; and adding a poached egg to his order, he proceeded musingly to shake some white sugar into his coffee, thinking all the time about Flambeau. He remembered how Flambeau had escaped, once by a pair of nail scissors, and once by a house on fire; once by having to pay for an unstamped letter, and once by getting people to look through a telescope at a comet that might destroy the world. He thought his detective brain as good as the criminal's, which was true. But he fully realized the disadvantage. "The criminal is the creative artist; the detective only the critic," he said with a sour smile, and lifted his coffee cup to his lips slowly, and put it down very quickly. He had put salt in it.

He looked at the vessel from which the silvery powder had come; it was certainly a sugar-basin; as unmistakably meant for sugar as a champagne-bottle for champagne. He wondered why they should keep salt in it. He looked to see if there were any more orthodox vessels. Yes, there were two salt-cellars quite full. Perhaps there was some speciality in the condiment in the salt-cellars. He tasted it; it was sugar. Then he looked round at the restaurant with a refreshed air of interest, to see if there were any other traces of that singular artistic taste which puts the sugar in the salt-cellars and the salt in the sugar-basin. Except for an odd splash of some dark fluid on one of the white-papered walls, the whole place appeared neat, cheerful and ordinary. He rang the bell for the waiter.

When that official hurried up, fuzzy-haired and somewhat blear-eyed at that early hour, the detective (who was not without an appreciation of the simpler forms of humour) asked him to taste the sugar and see if it was up to the high reputation of the hotel. The result was that the waiter yawned suddenly and woke up.

"Do you play this delicate joke on your customers every morning?" inquired Valentin. "Does changing the salt and sugar never pall on you as a jest?"

The waiter, when this irony grew clearer, stammeringly assured him that the establishment had certainly no such intention; it must be a most curious mistake. He picked up the sugar-basin and looked at it; he picked up the salt-cellar and looked at that, his face growing more and more bewildered. At last he abruptly excused himself, and hurrying away, returned in a few seconds with the proprietor. The proprietor also examined the sugar-basin and then the salt-cellar; the proprietor also looked bewildered.

Suddenly the waiter seemed to grow inarticulate with a rush of words.

"I zink," he stuttered eagerly, "I zink it is those two clergymen."

"What two clergymen?"

"The two clergymen," said the waiter, "that threw soup at the wall."

"Threw soup at the wall?" repeated Valentin, feeling sure this must be some Italian metaphor.

"Yes, yes," said the attendant excitedly, and pointing at the dark splash on the white paper; "threw it over there on the wall."

Valentin looked his query at the proprietor, who came to his rescue with fuller reports.

"Yes, sir," he said, "it's quite true, though I don't suppose it has anything to do with the sugar and salt. Two clergymen came in and drank soup here very early, as soon as the shutters were taken down. They were both very quiet, respectable people; one of them paid the bill and went out; the other, who seemed a slower coach altogether, was some minutes longer getting his things together. But he went at last. Only, the instant before he stepped into the street he deliberately picked up his cup, which he had only half emptied, and threw the soup slap on the wall. I was in the back room myself, and so was the waiter; so I could only rush out in time to find the wall splashed and the shop empty. It didn't do any particular damage, but it was confounded cheek; and I tried to catch the men in the street. They were too far off though; I only noticed they went round the corner into Carstairs Street."

The detective was on his feet, hat settled and stick in hand. He had already decided that in the universal darkness of his mind he could only follow the first odd finger that pointed; and this finger was odd enough. Paying his bill and clashing the glass doors behind him, he was soon swinging round into the other street.

It was fortunate that even in such fevered moments his eye was cool and quick. Something in a shop-front went by him like a mere flash; yet he went back to look at it. The shop was a popular greengrocer and fruiterer's, an array of goods set out in the open air and plainly ticketed with their names and prices. In the two most prominent compartments were two heaps, of oranges and of nuts respectively. On the heap of nuts lay a scrap of cardboard, on which was written in bold, blue chalk, "Best tangerine oranges, two a penny." On the oranges was the equally clear and exact description, "Finest Brazil nuts, 4d. a lb." M. Valentin looked at these two placards and fancied he had met this highly subtle form of humour before, and that somewhat recently. He drew the attention of the red-faced fruiterer, who was looking rather sullenly up and down the street, to this inaccuracy in his advertisements. The fruiterer said nothing, but sharply put each card into its proper place. The detective, leaning elegantly on his walking-cane, continued to scrutinize the shop. At last he said: "Pray excuse my apparent irrelevance, my good sir, but I should like to ask you a question in experimental psychology and the association of ideas."

The red-faced shopman regarded him with an eye of menace; but he continued gaily, swinging his cane. "Why," he pursued, "why are two tickets wrongly placed in a greengrocer's shop like a shovel hat that has come to London for a holiday? Or, in case I do not make myself clear, what is the mystical association which connects the idea of nuts marked as oranges with the idea of two clergymen, one tall and the other short?"

The eyes of the tradesman stood out of his head like a snail's; he really seemed for an instant likely to fling himself upon the stranger. At last he stammered angrily: "I don't know what you 'ave to do with it, but if you're one of their friends, you can tell 'em from me that I'll knock their silly 'eads off, parsons or no parsons, if they upset my apples again."

"Indeed?" asked the detective, with great sympathy. "Did they upset your apples?"

"One of 'em did," said the heated shopman; "rolled 'em all over the street. I'd 'ave caught the fool but for havin' to pick 'em up."

"Which way did these parsons go?" asked Valentin.

"Up that second road on the left-hand side, and then across the square," said the other promptly.

"Thanks," said Valentin, and vanished like a fairy. On the other side of the second square he found a policeman, and said: "This is urgent, constable; have you seen two clergymen in shovel hats?"

The policeman began to chuckle heavily. "I 'ave, sir; and if you arst me, one of 'em was drunk. He stood in the middle of the road that bewildered that——"

"Which way did they go?" snapped Valentin.

"They took one of them yellow buses over there," answered the man; "them that go to Hampstead."

Valentin produced his official card and said very rapidly: "Call up two of your men to come with me in pursuit," and crossed the road with such contagious energy that the ponderous policeman was moved to almost agile obedience. In a minute and a half the French detective was joined on the opposite pavement by an inspector and a man in plain clothes.

"Well, sir," began the former, with smiling importance, "and what may——?"

Valentin pointed suddenly with his cane. "I'll tell you on the top of that omnibus," he said, and was darting and dodging across the tangle of the traffic. When all three sank panting on the top seats of the yellow vehicle, the inspector said: "We could go four times as quick in a taxi."

"Quite true," replied their leader placidly, "if we only had an idea of where we were going."

"Well, where *are* you going?" asked the other, staring.

Valentin smoked frowningly for a few seconds; then, removing his cigarette, he said: "If you *know* what a man's doing, get in front of him; but if you want to guess what he's doing, keep behind him. Stray when he strays; stop when he stops; travel as slowly as he. Then you may see what he saw and may act as he acted. All we can do is to keep our eyes skinned for a queer thing."

"What sort of a queer thing do you mean?" asked the inspector.

"Any sort of queer thing," answered Valentin, and relapsed into obstinate silence.

The yellow omnibus crawled up the northern roads for what seemed like hours on end; the great detective would not explain further, and perhaps his assistants felt a silent and growing doubt of his errand. Perhaps, also, they felt a silent and growing desire for lunch, for the hours crept long past the normal luncheon hour, and the long roads of the North London suburbs seemed to shoot out into length after length like an infernal telescope. It was one of those journeys on which a man perpetually feels that now at last he must have come to the end of the universe, and then finds he has only come to the beginning of Tufnell Park. London died away in draggled taverns and dreary scrubs, and then was unaccountably born again in blazing high streets and blatant hotels. It was like passing through thirteen separate vulgar cities all just touching each other. But though the winter twilight was already threatening the road ahead of them, the Parisian detective still sat silent and watchful, eyeing the frontage of the streets that slid by on either side. By the time they had left Camden Town behind, the policemen were nearly asleep; at least, they gave something like a jump as Valentin leapt erect, struck a hand on each man's shoulder, and shouted to the driver to stop.

They tumbled down the steps into the road without realizing why they had been dislodged; when they looked round for enlightenment they found Valentin triumphantly pointing his finger towards a window on the left side of the road. It was a large window, forming part of the long façade of a gilt and palatial public-house; it was the part reserved for respectable dining, and labelled "Restaurant." This window, like all the rest along the frontage of the hotel, was of frosted and figured glass, but in the middle of it was a big, black smash, like a star in the ice.

"Our cue at last," cried Valentin, waving his stick; "the place with the broken window."

"What window? What cue?" asked his principal assistant. "Why, what proof is there that this has anything to do with them?"

Valentin almost broke his bamboo stick with rage.

"Proof!" he cried. "Good God! the man is looking for proof! Why, of course, the chances are twenty to one that it has *nothing* to do with them. But what else can we do? Don't you see we must either follow one wild possibility or else go home to bed?" He banged his way into the restaurant, followed by his companions, and they were soon seated at a late luncheon at a little table, and looking at the star of smashed glass from the inside. Not that it was very informative to them even then.

"Got your window broken, I see," said Valentin to the waiter, as he paid his bill.

"Yes, sir," answered the attendant, bending busily over the change, to which Valentin silently added an enormous tip. The waiter straightened himself with mild but unmistakable animation.

"Ah, yes, sir," he said. "Very odd thing, that, sir."

"Indeed? Tell us about it," said the detective with careless curiosity.

"Well, two gents in black came in," said the waiter; "two of those foreign parsons that are running about. They had a cheap and quiet little lunch, and one of them paid for it and went out. The other was just going out to join him when I looked at my change again and found he'd paid me more than three times too much. 'Here,' I says to the chap who was nearly out of the door, 'you've paid too much.' 'Oh,' he says, very cool, 'have we?' 'Yes,' I says, and picks up the bill to show him. Well, that was a knock-out."

"What do you mean?" asked his interlocutor.

"Well, I'd have sworn on seven Bibles that I'd put 4s. on that bill. But now I saw I'd put 14s., as plain as paint."

"Well?" cried Valentin, moving slowly, but with burning eyes, "and then?"

"The parson at the door he says, all serene, 'Sorry to confuse your accounts, but it'll pay for the window.' 'What window?' I says. 'The one I'm going to break,' he says, and smashed that blessed pane with his umbrella."

All the inquirers made an exclamation; and the inspector said under his breath: "Are we after escaped lunatics?" The waiter went on with some relish for the ridiculous story:

"I was so knocked silly for a second, I couldn't do anything. The man marched out of the place and joined his friend just round the corner. Then they went so quick up Bullock Street that I couldn't catch them, though I ran round the bars to do it."

"Bullock Street," said the detective, and shot up that thoroughfare as quickly as the strange couple he pursued.

Their journey now took them through bare brick ways like tunnels; streets with few lights and even with few windows; streets that seemed built out of the blank backs of everything and everywhere. Dusk was deepening, and it was not easy even for the London policemen to guess in what exact direction they were treading. The inspector, however, was pretty certain that they would eventually strike some part of Hampstead Heath. Abruptly one bulging and gas-lit window broke the blue twilight like a bull's-eye lantern; and Valentin stopped an instant before a little garish sweetstuff shop. After an instant's hesitation he went in; he stood amid the gaudy colours of the confectionery with entire gravity and bought thirteen chocolate cigars with a certain care. He was clearly preparing an opening; but he did not need one.

An angular, elderly young woman in the shop had regarded his elegant appearance with a merely automatic inquiry; but when she saw the door behind him blocked with the blue uniform of the inspector, her eyes seemed to wake up.

"Oh," she said, "if you've come about that parcel, I've sent it off already."

"Parcel!" repeated Valentin; and it was his turn to look inquiring.

"I mean the parcel the gentleman left—the clergyman gentleman."

"For goodness' sake," said Valentin, leaning forward with his first real confession of eagerness, "for Heaven's sake tell us what happened exactly."

"Well," said the woman, a little doubtfully, "the clergymen came in about half an hour ago and bought some peppermints and talked a bit, and then went off towards the Heath. But a second after, one of them runs back into the shop and says, 'Have I left a parcel?' Well, I looked everywhere and couldn't see one; so he says, 'Never mind; but if it should turn up, please post it to this address,' and he left me the address and a shilling for my trouble. And sure enough, though I thought I'd looked everywhere, I found he'd left a brown-paper parcel, so I posted it to the place he said. I can't remember the address now; it was somewhere in Westminster. But as the thing seemed so important, I thought perhaps the police had come about it."

"So they have," said Valentin shortly. "Is Hampstead Heath near here?"

"Straight on for fifteen minutes," said the woman, "and you'll come right out on the open." Valentin sprang out of the shop and began to run. The other detectives followed him at a reluctant trot.

The street they threaded was so narrow and shut in by shadows that when they came out unexpectedly into the void common and vast sky they were startled to find the evening still so light and clear. A perfect dome of peacock-green sank into gold amid the blackening trees and the dark violet distances. The glowing green tint was just deep enough to pick out in points of crystal one or two stars. All that was left of the daylight lay in a golden glitter across the edge of Hampstead and that popular hollow which is called the Vale of Health. The holiday makers who roam this region had not wholly dispersed: a few couples sat shapelessly on benches; and here and there a distant girl still shrieked in one of the swings. The glory of heaven deepened and darkened around the sublime vulgarity of man; and standing on the slope and looking across the valley, Valentin beheld the thing which he sought.

Among the black and breaking groups in that distance was one especially black which did not break—a group of two figures clerically clad. Though they seemed as small as insects, Valentin could see that one of them was much smaller than the other. Though the other had a student's stoop and an inconspicuous manner, he could see that the man was well over six feet high. He shut his teeth and went forward, whirling his stick impatiently. By the time he had substantially diminished the distance and magnified the two black figures as in a vast microscope, he had perceived something else; something which startled him, and yet which he had somehow expected. Whoever was the tall priest, there could be no doubt about the identity of the short one. It was his friend of the Harwich train, the stumpy little *curé* of Essex whom he had warned about his brown-paper parcels.

Now, so far as this went, everything fitted in finally and rationally enough. Valentin had learned by his inquiries that morning that a Father Brown from Essex was bringing up a silver cross with sapphires, a relic of considerable value, to show some of the foreign priests at the congress. This undoubtedly was the "silver with blue stones"; and Father Brown undoubtedly was the little greenhorn in the train. Now there was nothing wonderful about the fact that what Valentin had found out Flambeau had also found out; Flambeau found out everything. Also there was nothing wonderful in the fact that when Flambeau heard of a sapphire cross he should try to steal it; that was the most natural thing in all natural history. And most certainly there was nothing wonderful about the fact that Flambeau should have it all his own way with such a silly sheep as the man with the umbrella and the parcels. He was the sort of man whom anybody could lead on a string to the North Pole; it was not surprising that an actor like Flambeau, dressed as another priest, could lead him to Hampstead Heath. So far the crime seemed clear enough; and while the detective pitied the priest for his helplessness, he almost despised Flambeau for condescending to so gullible a victim. But when Valentin thought of all that had happened in between, of all that had led him to his triumph, he racked his brains for the smallest rhyme or reason in it. What had the stealing of a blue-and-silver cross from a priest from Essex to do with chucking soup at wallpaper? What had it to do with calling nuts oranges, or with paying for windows first and breaking them afterwards? He had come to the end of his chase; yet somehow he had missed the middle of it. When he failed (which was seldom), he had usually grasped the clue, but nevertheless missed the criminal. Here he had grasped the criminal, but still he could not grasp the clue.

The two figures that they followed were crawling like black flies across the huge green contour of a hill. They were evidently sunk in conversation, and perhaps did not notice where they were going; but they were certainly going to the wilder and more silent heights of the Heath. As their pursuers gained on them, the latter had to use the undignified attitudes of the deer-stalker, to crouch behind clumps of trees and even to crawl prostrate in deep grass. By these ungainly ingenuities the hunters even came close enough to the quarry to hear the murmur of the discussion, but no word could be distinguished except the word "reason" recurring frequently in a high and almost childish voice. Once, over an abrupt dip of land and a dense tangle of thickets, the detectives actually lost the two figures they were following. They did not find the trail again for an agonizing ten minutes, and then it led round the brow of a great dome of hill overlooking an amphitheatre of rich and desolate sunset scenery. Under a tree in this commanding yet neglected spot was an old ramshackle wooden seat. On this seat sat the two priests still in serious speech together. The gorgeous green and gold still clung to the darkening horizon; but the dome above was turning slowly from peacock-green to peacock-blue, and the stars detached themselves more and more like solid jewels. Mutely motioning to his followers, Valentin contrived to creep up behind the big branching tree, and, standing there in deathly silence, heard the words of the strange priests for the first time.

After he had listened for a minute and a half, he was gripped by a devilish doubt. Perhaps he had dragged the two English policemen to the wastes of a nocturnal heath on an errand no saner than seeking figs on thistles. For the two priests were talking exactly like priests, piously, with learning and leisure, about the most aerial enigmas of theology. The little Essex priest spoke the more simply, with his round face turned to the strengthening stars; the other talked with his head bowed, as if he were not even worthy to look at them. But no more innocently clerical conversation could have been heard in any white Italian cloister or black Spanish cathedral.

The first he heard was the tail of one of Father Brown's sentences, which ended: ". . . what they really meant in the Middle Ages by the heavens being incorruptible."

The taller priest nodded his bowed head and said:

"Ah, yes, these modern infidels appeal to their reason; but who can look at those millions of worlds and not feel that there may well be wonderful universes above us where reason is utterly unreasonable?"

"No," said the other priest; "reason is always reasonable, even in the last limbo, in the lost borderland of things. I know that people charge the Church with lowering reason, but it is just the other way. Alone on earth, the Church makes reason really supreme. Alone on earth, the Church affirms that God Himself is bound by reason."

The other priest raised his austere face to the spangled sky and said: "Yet who knows if in that infinite universe——?"

"Only infinite physically," said the little priest, turning sharply in his seat, "not infinite in the sense of escaping from the laws of truth."

Valentin behind his tree was tearing his finger-nails with silent fury. He seemed almost to hear the sniggers of the English detectives whom he had brought so far on a fantastic guess only to listen to the metaphysical gossip of two mild old parsons. In his impatience he lost the equally elaborate answer of the tall cleric, and when he listened again it was again Father Brown who was speaking:

"Reason and justice grip the remotest and the loneliest star. Look at those stars. Don't they look as if they were single diamonds and sapphires? Well, you can imagine any mad botany or geology you please. Think of forests of adamant with leaves of brilliants. Think the moon is a blue moon, a single elephantine sapphire. But don't fancy that all that frantic astronomy would make the smallest difference to the reason and justice of conduct. On plains of opal, under cliffs cut out of pearl, you would still find a notice-board, 'Thou shalt not steal.' "

Valentin was just in the act of rising from his rigid and crouching attitude and creeping away as softly as might be, felled by the one great folly of his life. But something in the very silence of the tall priest made him stop until the latter spoke. When at last he did speak, he said simply, his head bowed and his hands on his knees:

"Well, I still think that other worlds may perhaps rise higher than our reason. The mystery of heaven is unfathomable, and I for one can only bow my head."

Then, with brow yet bent and without changing by the faintest shade his attitude or voice, he added:

"Just hand over that sapphire cross of yours, will you? We're all alone here, and I could pull you to pieces like a straw doll."

The utterly unaltered voice and attitude added a strange violence to that shocking change of speech. But the guarder of the relic only seemed to turn his head by the smallest section of the compass. He seemed still to have a somewhat foolish face turned to the stars. Perhaps he had not understood. Or, perhaps, he had understood and sat rigid with terror.

"Yes," said the tall priest, in the same low voice and in the same still posture, "yes, I am Flambeau."

Then, after a pause, he said:

"Come, will you give me that cross?"

"No," said the other, and the monosyllable had an odd sound.

Flambeau suddenly flung off all his pontifical pretensions. The great robber leaned back in his seat and laughed low but long.

"No," he cried; "you won't give it me, you proud prelate. You won't give it me, you little celibate simpleton. Shall I tell you why you won't give it me? Because I've got it already in my own breast-pocket."

The small man from Essex turned what seemed to be a dazed face in the dusk, and said, with the timid eagerness of "The Private Secretary":

"Are—are you sure?"

Flambeau yelled with delight.

"Really, you're as good as a three-act farce," he cried. "Yes, you turnip, I am quite sure. I had the sense to make a duplicate of the right parcel, and now, my friend, you've got the duplicate, and I've got the jewels. An old dodge, Father Brown—a very old dodge."

"Yes," said Father Brown, and passed his hand through his hair with the same strange vagueness of manner. "Yes, I've heard of it before."

The colossus of crime leaned over to the little rustic priest with a sort of sudden interest.

"*You* have heard of it?" he asked. "Where have *you* heard of it?"

"Well, I mustn't tell you his name, of course," said the little man simply. "He was a penitent, you know. He had lived prosperously for about twenty years entirely on duplicate brown-paper parcels. And so, you see, when I began to suspect you, I thought of this poor chap's way of doing it at once."

"Began to suspect me?" repeated the outlaw with increased intensity. "Did you really have the gumption to suspect me just because I brought you up to this bare part of the heath?"

"No, no," said Brown with an air of apology. "You see, I suspected you when we first met. It's that little bulge up the sleeve where you people have the spiked bracelet."

"How in Tartarus," cried Flambeau, "did you ever hear of the spiked bracelet?"

"Oh, one's little flock, you know!" said Father Brown, arching his eyebrows rather blankly. "When I was a curate in Hartlepool, there were three of them with spiked bracelets. So, as I suspected you from the first, don't you see, I made sure that the cross should go safe, anyhow. I'm afraid I watched you, you know. So at last I saw you change the parcels. Then, don't you see, I changed them back again. And then I left the right one behind."

"Left it behind?" repeated Flambeau, and for the first time there was another note in his voice beside his triumph.

"Well, it was like this," said the little priest, speaking in the same unaffected way. "I went back to that sweet-shop and asked if I'd left a parcel, and gave them a particular address if it turned up. Well, I knew I hadn't; but when I went away again I did. So, instead of running after me with that valuable parcel, they have sent it flying to a friend of mine in Westminster." Then he added rather sadly: "I learnt that, too, from a poor fellow in Hartlepool. He used to do it with handbags he stole at railway stations, but he's in a monastery now. Oh, one gets to know, you know," he added, rubbing his head again with the same sort of desperate apology. "We can't help being priests. People come and tell us these things."

Flambeau tore a brown-paper parcel out of his inner pocket and rent it in pieces. There was nothing but paper and sticks of lead inside it. He sprang to his feet with a gigantic gesture, and cried:

"I don't believe you. I don't believe a bumpkin like you could manage all that. I believe you've still got the stuff on you, and if you don't give it up—why, we're all alone, and I'll take it by force!"

"No," said Father Brown simply, and stood up also; "you won't take it by force. First, because I really haven't still got it. And, second, because we are not alone."

Flambeau stopped in his stride forward.

"Behind that tree," said Father Brown, pointing, "are two strong policemen and the greatest detective alive. How did they come here, do you ask? Why, I brought them, of course! How did I do it? Why, I'll tell you if you like! Lord bless you, we have to know twenty such things when we work among the criminal classes! Well, I wasn't sure you were a thief, and it would never do to make a scandal against one of our own clergy. So I just tested you to see if anything would make you show yourself. A man generally makes a small scene if he finds salt in his coffee; if he doesn't, he has some reason for keeping quiet. I changed the salt and sugar, and *you* kept quiet. A man generally objects if his bill is three times too big. If he pays it, he has some motive for passing unnoticed. I altered your bill, and *you* paid it."

The world seemed waiting for Flambeau to leap like a tiger. But he was held back as by a spell; he was stunned with the utmost curiosity.

"Well," went on Father Brown, with lumbering lucidity, "as you wouldn't leave any tracks for the police, of course somebody had to. At every place we went to, I took care to do something that would get us talked about for the rest of the day. I didn't do much harm—a splashed wall, spilt apples, a broken window; but I saved the cross, as the cross will always be saved. It is at Westminster by now. I rather wonder you didn't stop it with the Donkey's Whistle."

"With the what?" asked Flambeau.

"I'm glad you've never heard of it," said the priest, making a face. "It's a foul thing. I'm sure you're too good a man for a Whistler. I couldn't have countered it even with the Spots myself; I'm not strong enough in the legs."

"What on earth are you talking about?" asked the other.

"Well, I did think you'd know the Spots," said Father Brown, agreeably surprised. "Oh, you can't have gone so very wrong yet!"

"How in blazes do you know all these horrors?" cried Flambeau.

The shadow of a smile crossed the round, simple face of his clerical opponent.

"Oh, by being a celibate simpleton, I suppose," he said. "Has it never struck you that a man who does next to nothing but hear men's real sins is not likely to be wholly unaware of human evil? But, as a matter of fact, another part of my trade, too, made me sure you weren't a priest."

"What?" asked the thief, almost gaping.

"You attacked reason," said Father Brown. "It's bad theology."

And even as he turned away to collect his property, the three policemen came out from under the twilight trees. Flambeau was an artist and a sportsman. He stepped back and swept Valentin a great bow.

"Do not bow to me, *mon ami*," said Valentin, with silver clearness. "Let us both bow to our master."

And they both stood an instant uncovered, while the little Essex priest blinked about for his umbrella.

The Sins of Prince Saradine

When Flambeau took his month's holiday from his office in Westminster he took it in a small sailing-boat, so small that it passed much of its time as a rowing-boat. He took it, moreover, on little rivers in the Eastern counties, rivers so small that the boat looked like a magic boat sailing on land through meadows and cornfields. The vessel was just comfortable for two people; there was room only for necessities, and Flambeau had stocked it with such things as his special philosophy considered necessary. They reduced themselves, apparently, to four essentials: tins of salmon, if he should want to eat; loaded revolvers, if he should want to fight; a bottle of brandy, presumably in case he should faint; and a priest, presumably in case he should die. With this light luggage he crawled down the little Norfolk rivers, intending to reach the Broads at last, but meanwhile delighting in the over-hanging gardens and meadows, the mirrored mansions or villages, lingering to fish in the pools and corners, and in some sense hugging the shore.

Like a true philosopher, Flambeau had no aim in his holiday; but, like a true philosopher, he had an excuse. He had a sort of half purpose, which he took just so seriously that its success would crown the holiday, but just so lightly that its failure would not spoil it. Years ago, when he had been a king of thieves and the most famous figure in Paris, he had often received wild communications of approval, denunciation or even love; but one had, somehow, stuck in his memory. It consisted simply of a visiting-card, in an envelope with an English postmark. On the back of the card was written in French and in green ink: "If you ever retire and become respectable, come and see me. I want to meet you, for I have met all the other great men of my time. That trick of yours of getting one detective to arrest the other was the most splendid scene in French history." On the front of the card was engraved in the formal fashion, "Prince Saradine, Reed House, Reed Island, Norfolk."

He had not troubled much about the prince then, beyond ascertaining that he had been a brilliant and fashionable figure in southern Italy. In his youth, it was said, he had eloped with a married woman of high rank; the escapade was scarcely startling in his social world, but it had clung to men's minds because of an additional tragedy: the alleged suicide of the insulted husband, who appeared to have flung himself over a precipice in Sicily. The prince then lived in Vienna for a time, but his more recent years seemed to have been passed in perpetual and restless travel. But when Flambeau, like the prince himself, had left European celebrity and settled in England, it occurred to him that he might pay a surprise visit to this eminent exile in the Norfolk Broads. Whether he should find the place he had no idea; and, indeed, it was sufficiently small and forgotten. But, as things fell out, he found it much sooner than he expected.

They had moored their boat one night under a bank veiled in high grasses and short pollarded trees. Sleep, after heavy sculling, had come to them early, and by a corresponding accident they awoke before it was light. To speak more strictly, they awoke before it was daylight; for a large lemon moon was only just setting in the forest of high grass above their heads, and the sky was of a vivid violet-blue, nocturnal but bright. Both men had simultaneously a reminiscence of childhood, of the elfin and adventurous time when tall weeds close over us like woods. Standing up thus against the large low moon the daisies really seemed to be giant daisies, the dandelions to be giant dandelions. Somehow it reminded them of the dado of a nursery wall-paper. The drop of the river-bed sufficed to sink them under the roots of all shrubs and flowers and make them gaze upwards at the grass.

"By Jove!" said Flambeau; "it's like being in fairyland."

Father Brown sat bolt upright in the boat and crossed himself. His movement was so abrupt that his friend asked him, with a mild stare, what was the matter.

"The people who wrote the mediæval ballads," answered the priest, "knew more about fairies than you do. It isn't only nice things that happen in fairyland."

"Oh, bosh!" said Flambeau. "Only nice things could happen under such an innocent moon. I am for pushing on now and seeing what does really come. We may die and rot before we ever see again such a moon or such a mood."

"All right," said Father Brown. "I never said it was always wrong to enter fairyland. I only said it was always dangerous."

They pushed slowly up the brightening river; the glowing violet of the sky and the pale gold of the moon grew fainter and fainter, and faded into that vast colourless cosmos that precedes the colours of the dawn. When the first faint stripes of red and gold and grey split the horizon from end to end they were broken by the black bulk of a town or village which sat on the river just ahead of them. It was already an easy twilight, in which all things were visible, when they came under the hanging roofs and bridges of this riverside hamlet. The houses, with their long, low, stooping roofs, seemed to come down to drink at the river, like huge grey and red cattle. The broadening and whitening dawn had already turned to working daylight before they saw any living creature on the wharves and bridges of that silent town. Eventually they saw a very placid and prosperous man in his shirt sleeves, with a face as round as the recently sunken moon, and rays of red whisker around the low arc of it, who was leaning on a post above the sluggish tide. By an impulse not to be analysed, Flambeau rose to his full height in the swaying boat and shouted at the man to ask if he knew Reed Island or Reed House. The prosperous man's smile grew slightly more expansive, and he simply pointed up the river towards the next bend of it. Flambeau went ahead without further speech.

The boat took many such grassy corners and followed many such reedy and silent reaches of river; but before the search had become monotonous they had swung round a specially sharp angle and come into the silence of a sort of pool or lake, the sight of which instinctively arrested them. For in the middle of this wider piece of water, fringed on every side with rushes, lay a long, low islet along which ran a long, low house or bungalow built of bamboo or some kind of tough tropic cane. The upstanding rods of bamboo which made the walls were pale yellow, the sloping rods that made the roof were of darker red or brown, otherwise the long house was a thing of repetition and monotony. The early morning breeze rustled the reeds round the island and sang in the strange ribbed house as in a giant pan-pipe.

"By George!" cried Flambeau; "here is the place, after all! Here is Reed Island, if ever there was one. Here is Reed House, if it is anywhere. I believe that fat man with whiskers was a fairy."

"Perhaps," remarked Father Brown impartially. "If he was, he was a bad fairy."

But even as he spoke the impetuous Flambeau had run his boat ashore in the rattling reeds, and they stood on the long, quaint islet beside the old and silent house.

The house stood with its back, as it were, to the river and the only landing-stage; the main entrance was on the other side, and looked down the long island garden. The visitors approached it, therefore, by a small path running round nearly three sides of the house, close under the low eaves. Through three different windows on three different sides they looked in on the same long, well-lit room, panelled in light wood, with a large number of looking-glasses, and laid out as for an elegant lunch. The front door, when they came round to it at last, was flanked by two turquoise-blue flower-pots. It was opened by a butler of the drearier type— long, lean, grey and listless—who murmured that Prince Saradine was from home at present, but was expected hourly; the house being kept ready for him and his guests. The exhibition of the card with the scrawl of green ink awoke a flicker of life in the parchment face of this depressed retainer, and it was with a certain shaky courtesy that he suggested that the strangers should remain. "His Highness may be here any minute," he said, "and would be distressed to have just missed any gentleman he had invited. We have orders always to keep a little cold lunch for him and his friends, and I am sure he would wish it to be offered."

Moved with curiosity to this minor adventure, Flambeau assented gracefully, and followed the old man, who ushered him ceremoniously into the long, lightly panelled room. There was nothing very notable about it, except the rather unusual alternation of many long, low windows with many long, low oblongs of looking-glass, which gave a singular air of lightness and unsubstantialness to the place. It was somehow like lunching out of doors. One or two pictures of a quiet kind hung in the corners: one a large grey photograph of a very young man in uniform, another a red chalk sketch of two long-haired boys. Asked by Flambeau whether the soldierly person was the prince, the butler answered shortly in the negative; it was the prince's younger brother, Captain Stephen Saradine, he said. And with that the old man seemed to dry up suddenly and lose all taste for conversation.

After lunch had tailed off with exquisite coffee and liqueurs, the guests were introduced to the garden, the library, and the housekeeper—a dark handsome lady, of no little majesty, and rather like a plutonic Madonna. It appeared that she and the butler were the only survivors of the prince's original foreign *ménage*, all the other servants now in the house being new and collected in Norfolk by the housekeeper. This latter lady went by the name of Mrs. Anthony, but she spoke with a slight Italian accent, and Flambeau did not doubt that Anthony was a Norfolk version of some more Latin name. Mr. Paul, the butler, also had a faintly foreign air, but he was in tongue and training English, as are many of the most polished men-servants of the cosmopolitan nobility.

Pretty and unique as it was, the place had about it a curious luminous sadness. Hours passed in it like days. The long, well-windowed rooms were full of daylight, but it seemed a dead daylight. And through all other incidental noises, the sound of talk, the clink of glasses, or the passing feet of servants, they could hear on all sides of the house the melancholy noise of the river.

"We have taken a wrong turning and come to a wrong place," said Father Brown, looking out of the window at the grey-green sedges and the silver flood. "Never mind; one can sometimes do good by being the right person in the wrong place."

Father Brown, though commonly a silent, was an oddly sympathetic little man, and in those few but endless hours he unconsciously sank deeper into the secrets of Reed House than his professional friend. He had that knack of friendly silence which is so essential to gossip; and saying scarcely a word, he probably obtained from his new acquaintances all that in any case they would have told. The butler indeed was naturally uncommunicative. He betrayed a sullen and almost animal affection for his master, who, he said, had been very badly treated. The chief offender seemed to be his highness's brother, whose name alone would lengthen the old man's lantern jaws and pucker his parrot nose into a sneer. Captain Stephen was a ne'er-do-well, apparently, and had drained his benevolent brother of hundreds and thousands; forced him to fly from fashionable life and live quietly in this retreat. That was all Paul, the butler, would say, and Paul was obviously a partisan.

The Italian housekeeper was somewhat more communicative, being, as Brown fancied, somewhat less content. Her tone about her master was faintly acid, though not without a certain awe. Flambeau and his friend were standing in the room of the looking-glasses examining the red sketch of the two boys when the housekeeper swept in swiftly on some domestic errand. It was a peculiarity of this glittering, glass-panelled place that anyone entering was reflected in four or five mirrors at once; and Father Brown, without turning round, stopped in the middle of a sentence of family criticism. But Flambeau, who had his face close up to the picture, was already saying in a loud voice: "The brothers Saradine, I suppose. They both look innocent enough. It would be hard to say which is the good brother and which the bad." Then realizing the lady's presence, he turned the conversation with some triviality, and strolled out into the garden. But Father Brown still gazed steadily at the red crayon sketch; and Mrs. Anthony still gazed steadily at Father Brown.

She had large and tragic brown eyes, and her olive face glowed darkly with a curious and painful wonder—as of one doubtful of a stranger's identity or purpose. Whether the little priest's coat and creed touched some southern memories of confession, or whether she fancied he knew more than he did, she said to him in a low voice, as to a fellow plotter: "He is right enough in one way, your friend. He says it would be hard to pick out the good and bad brothers. Oh, it would be hard, it would be mighty hard, to pick out the good one."

"I don't understand you," said Father Brown, and began to move away.

The woman took a step nearer to him, with thunderous brows and a sort of savage stoop, like a bull lowering his horns.

"There isn't a good one," she hissed. "There was badness enough in the captain taking all that money, but I don't think there was much goodness in the prince giving it. The captain's not the only man with something against him."

A light dawned on the cleric's averted face, and his mouth formed silently the word "blackmail." Even as he did so the woman turned an abrupt white face over her shoulder and almost fell. The door had opened soundlessly and the pale Paul stood like a ghost in the doorway. By the weird trick of the reflecting walls, it seemed as if five Pauls had entered by five doors simultaneously.

"His Highness," he said, "has just arrived."

In the same flash the figure of a man had passed outside the first window, crossing the sunlit pane like a lighted stage. An instant later he passed at the second window, and the many mirrors repainted in successive frames the same eagle profile and marching figure. He was erect and alert, but his hair was white and his complexion of an odd ivory yellow. He had that short, curved Roman nose which generally goes with long, lean cheeks and chin, but these were partly masked by moustache and imperial. The moustache was much darker than the beard, giving an effect slightly theatrical, and he was dressed up to the same dashing part, having a white top hat, an orchid in his coat, a yellow waistcoat and yellow gloves which he flapped and swung as he walked. When he came round to the front door they heard the stiff Paul open it, and heard the new arrival say cheerfully: "Well, you see I have come." The stiff Mr. Paul bowed and answered in his inaudible manner; for a few minutes their conversation could not be heard. Then the butler said: "Everything is at your disposal"; and the glove-flapping Prince Saradine came gaily into the room to greet them. They beheld once more that spectral scene—five princes entering a room with five doors.

The prince put the white hat and yellow gloves on the table and offered his hand quite cordially.

"Delighted to see you here, Mr. Flambeau," he said. "Know you very well by reputation, if that's not an indiscreet remark."

"Not at all," answered Flambeau, laughing. "I am not sensitive. Very few reputations are gained by unsullied virtue."

The prince flashed a sharp look at him to see if the retort had any personal point; then he laughed also and offered chairs to everyone, including himself.

"Pleasant little place this, I think," he said with a detached air. "Not much to do, I fear; but the fishing is really good."

The priest, who was staring at him with the grave stare of a baby, was haunted by some fancy that escaped definition. He looked at the grey, carefully curled hair, yellow-white visage, and slim, somewhat foppish figure. These were not unnatural, though perhaps a shade *prononcé*, like the outfit of a figure behind the footlights. The nameless interest lay in something else, in the very framework of the face; Brown was tormented with a half memory of having seen it somewhere before. The man looked like some old friend of his dressed up. Then he remembered the mirrors, and put his fancy down to some psychological effect of that multiplication of human masks.

Prince Saradine distributed his social attentions between his guests with great gaiety and tact. Finding the detective of a sporting turn and eager to employ his holiday, he guided Flambeau and Flambeau's boat down to the best fishing spot in the stream, and was back in his own canoe in twenty minutes to join Father Brown in the library and plunge equally politely into the priest's more philosophic pleasures. He seemed to know a great deal both about the fishing and the books, though of these not the most edifying; he spoke five or six languages, though chiefly the slang of each. He had evidently lived in varied cities and very motley societies, for some of his cheerfullest stories were about gambling hells and opium dens, Australian bushrangers or Italian brigands. Father Brown knew that the once celebrated Saradine had spent his last few years in almost ceaseless travel, but he had not guessed that the travels were so disreputable or so amusing.

Indeed, with all his dignity of a man of the world, Prince Saradine radiated, to such sensitive observers as the priest, a certain atmosphere of the restless and even the unreliable. His face was fastidious, but his eye was wild; he had little nervous tricks, like a man shaken by drink or drugs; and he neither had, nor professed to have, his hand on the helm of household affairs. All these were left to the two old servants, especially to the butler, who was plainly the central pillar of the house. Mr. Paul, indeed, was not so much a butler as a sort of steward, or even, chamberlain; he dined privately, but with almost as much pomp as his master; he was feared by all the servants; and he consulted with the prince decorously, but somewhat unbendingly—rather as if he were the prince's solicitor. The sombre housekeeper was a mere shadow in comparison; indeed, she seemed to efface herself and wait only on the butler, and Brown heard no more of those volcanic whispers which had half told him of the younger brother who blackmailed the elder. Whether the prince was really being thus bled by the absent captain he could not be certain, but there was something insecure and secretive about Saradine that made the tale by no means incredible.

When they went once more into the long hall with the windows and the mirrors yellow evening was dropping over the waters and the willowy banks, and a bittern sounded in the distance like an elf upon his dwarfish drum. The same singular sentiment of some sad and evil fairyland crossed the priest's mind again like a grey cloud. "I wish Flambeau were back," he muttered.

"Do you believe in doom?" asked the restless Prince Saradine suddenly.

"No," answered his guest. "I believe in Doomsday."

The prince turned from the window and stared at him in a singular manner, his face in shadow against the sunset. "What do you mean?" he asked.

"I mean that we here are on the wrong side of the tapestry," answered Father Brown. "The things that happen here do not seem to mean anything; they mean something somewhere else. Somewhere else retribution will come on the real offender. Here it often seems to fall on the wrong person."

The prince made an inexplicable noise like an animal; in his shadowed face the eyes were shining queerly. A new and shrewd thought exploded silently in the other's mind. Was there another meaning in Saradine's blend of brilliancy and abruptness? Was the prince—— Was he perfectly sane? He was repeating, "The wrong person—the wrong person," many more times than was natural in a social exclamation.

Then Father Brown awoke tardily to a second truth. In the mirrors before him he could see the silent door standing open, and the silent Mr. Paul standing in it, with his usual pallid impassiveness.

"I thought it better to announce at once," he said, with the same stiff respectfulness as of an old family lawyer, "a boat rowed by six men has come to the landing-stage, and there's a gentleman sitting in the stern."

"A boat!" repeated the prince; "a gentleman?" and he rose to his feet.

There was a startled silence punctuated only by the odd noise of the bird in the sedge; and then, before anyone could speak again, a new face and figure passed in profile round the three sunlit windows, as the prince had passed an hour or two before. But except for the accident that both outlines were aquiline, they had little in common. Instead of the new white topper of Saradine, was a black one of antiquated or foreign shape; under it was a young and very solemn face, clean shaven, blue about its resolute chin, and carrying a faint suggestion of the young Napoleon. The association was assisted by something old and odd about the whole get-up, as of a man who had never troubled to change the fashions of his fathers. He had a shabby blue frock coat, a red, soldierly looking waistcoat, and a kind of coarse white trousers common among the early

Victorians, but strangely incongruous to-day. From all this old clothes-shop his olive face stood out strangely young and monstrously sincere.

"The deuce!" said Prince Saradine, and clapping on his white hat he went to the front door himself, flinging it open on the sunset garden.

By that time the new-comer and his followers were drawn up on the lawn like a small stage army. The six boatmen had pulled the boat well up on shore, and were guarding it almost menacingly holding their oars erect like spears. They were swarthy men, and some of them wore earrings. But one of them stood forward beside the olive-faced young man in the red waistcoat, and carried a large black case of unfamiliar form.

"Your name," said the young man, "is Saradine?"

Saradine assented rather negligently.

The new-comer had dull, dog-like brown eyes, as different as possible from the restless and glittering grey eyes of the prince. But once again Father Brown was tortured with a sense of having seen somewhere a replica of the face; and once again he remembered the repetitions of the glass-panelled room, and put down the coincidence to that. "Confound this crystal palace!" he muttered. "One sees everything too many times. It's like a dream."

"If you are Prince Saradine," said the young man, "I may tell you that my name is Antonelli."

"Antonelli," repeated the prince languidly. "Somehow I remember the name."

"Permit me to present myself," said the young Italian.

With his left hand he politely took off his old-fashioned top hat; with his right he caught Prince Saradine so ringing a crack across the face that the white top hat rolled down the steps and one of the blue flower-pots rocked upon its pedestal.

The prince, whatever he was, was evidently not a coward; he sprang at his enemy's throat and almost bore him backwards to the grass. But his enemy extricated himself with a singularly inappropriate air of hurried politeness.

"That is all right," he said, panting and in halting English. "I have insulted. I will give satisfaction. Marco, open the case."

The man beside him with the earrings and the big black case proceeded to unlock it. He took out of it two long Italian rapiers, with splendid steel hilts and blades, which he planted point downwards in the lawn. The strange young man standing facing the entrance with his yellow and vindictive face, the two swords standing up in the turf like two crosses in a cemetery, and the line of the ranked rowers behind, gave it all an odd appearance of being some barbaric court of justice. But everything else was unchanged, so sudden had been the interruption. The sunset gold still glowed on the lawn, and the bittern still boomed as announcing some small but dreadful destiny.

"Prince Saradine," said the man called Antonelli; "when I was an infant in the cradle you killed my father and stole my mother; my father was the more fortunate. You did not kill him fairly, as I am going to kill you. You and my wicked mother took him driving to a lonely pass in Sicily, flung him down a cliff, and went on your way. I could imitate you if I chose, but imitating you is too vile. I have followed you all over the world, and you have always fled from me. But this is the end of the world—and of you. I have you now, and I give you the chance you never gave my father. Choose one of those swords."

Prince Saradine, with contracted brows, seemed to hesitate a moment, but his ears were still singing with the blow, and he sprang forward and snatched at one of the hilts. Father Brown had also sprung forward, striving to compose the dispute; but he soon found his personal presence made matters worse. Saradine was a French Freemason and a fierce atheist, and a priest moved him by the law of contraries. And for the other man neither priest nor layman moved him at all. This young man with the Bonaparte face and the brown eyes was something far sterner than a puritan—a pagan. He was a simple slayer from the morning of the earth; a man of the stone age—a man of stone.

One hope remained, the summoning of the household; and Father Brown ran back into the house. He found, however, that all the under-servants had been given a holiday ashore by the autocrat Paul, and that only the sombre Mrs. Anthony moved uneasily about the long rooms. But the moment she turned a ghastly face upon him, he resolved one of the riddles of the house of mirrors. The heavy brown eyes of Antonelli were the heavy brown eyes of Mrs. Anthony, and in a flash he saw half the story.

"Your son is outside," he said, without wasting words; "either he or the prince will be killed. Where is Mr. Paul?"

"He is at the landing-stage," said the woman faintly. "He is—he is—signalling for help."

"Mrs. Anthony," said Father Brown seriously, "there is no time for nonsense. My friend has his boat down the river, fishing. Your son's boat is guarded by your son's men. There is only this one canoe; what is Mr. Paul doing with it?"

"Santa Maria! I do not know," she said; and swooned all her length on the matted floor.

Father Brown lifted her to a sofa, flung a pot of water over her, shouted for help, and then rushed down to the landing-stage of the little island.

But the canoe was already in mid-stream, and old Paul was pulling and pushing it up the river with an energy incredible at his years.

"I will save my master," he cried, his eyes blazing maniacally. "I will save him yet!"

Father Brown could do nothing but gaze after the boat as it struggled up-stream, and pray that the old man might waken the little town in time.

"A duel is bad enough," he muttered, rubbing up his rough dust-coloured hair, "but there's something wrong about this duel, even as a duel. I feel it in my bones. But what can it be?"

As he stood staring at the water, a wavering mirror of sunset, he heard from the other end of the island garden a small but unmistakable sound—the cold concussion of steel. He turned his head.

Away on the farthest cape or headland of the long islet, on a strip of turf beyond the last rank of roses, the duellists had already crossed swords. Evening above them was a dome of virgin gold, and, distant as they were, every detail was picked out. They had cast off their coats, but the yellow waistcoat and white hair of Saradine, the red waistcoat and white trousers of Antonelli, glittered in the level light like the colours of the dancing clockwork dolls. The two swords sparkled from point to pommel like two diamond pins. There was something frightful in the two figures appearing so little and so gay. They looked like two butterflies trying to pin each other to a cork.

Father Brown ran as hard as he could, his little legs going like a wheel. But when he came to the field of combat he found he was both too late and too early—too late to stop the strife, under the shadow of the grim Sicilians leaning on their oars, and too early to anticipate any disastrous issue of it. For the two men were singularly well matched, the prince using his skill with a sort of cynical confidence, the Sicilian using his with a murderous care. Few finer fencing matches can ever have been seen in crowded amphitheatres than that which tinkled and sparkled on that forgotten island in the reedy river. The dizzy fight was balanced so long that hope began to revive in the protesting priest; by all common probability Paul must soon come back with the police. It would be some comfort even if Flambeau came back from his fishing, for Flambeau, physically speaking, was worth four other men. But there was no sign of Flambeau, and, what was much queerer, no sign of Paul or the police. No other raft or stick was left to float on; in that lost island in that vast nameless pool, they were cut off as on a rock in the Pacific.

Almost as he had the thought the ringing of the rapiers quickened to a rattle, the prince's arms flew up, and the point shot out behind between his shoulder-blades. He went over with a great whirling movement, almost like one throwing the half of a boy's cart-wheel. The sword flew from his hand like a shooting star, and dived into the distant river; and he himself sank with so earth-shaking a subsidence that he broke a big rose-tree with his body and shook up into the sky a cloud of red earth—like the smoke of some heathen sacrifice. The Sicilian had made blood-offering to the ghost of his father.

The priest was instantly on his knees by the corpse, but only to make too sure that it was a corpse. As he was still trying some last hopeless tests he heard for the first time voices from farther up the river, and saw a police-boat shoot up to the landing-stage with constables and other important people, including the excited Paul. The little priest rose with a distinctly dubious grimace.

"Now, why on earth," he muttered, "why on earth couldn't he have come before?"

Some seven minutes later the island was occupied by an invasion of townsfolk and police, and the latter had put their hands on the victorious duellist, ritually reminding him that anything he said might be used against him.

"I shall not say anything," said the monomaniac, with a wonderful and peaceful face. "I shall never say anything any more. I am very happy, and I only want to be hanged."

Then he shut his mouth as they led him away, and it is the strange but certain truth that he never opened it again in this world, except to say "Guilty" at his trial.

Father Brown had stared at the suddenly crowded garden, the arrest of the man of blood, the carrying away of the corpse after its examination by the doctor, rather as one watches the break-up of some ugly dream; he was motionless, like a man in a nightmare. He gave his name and address as a witness, but declined their offer of a boat to the shore, and remained alone in the island garden, gazing at the broken rose bush and the whole green theatre of that swift and inexplicable tragedy. The light died along the river; mist rose in the marshy banks; a few belated birds flitted fitfully across.

Stuck stubbornly in his sub-consciousness (which was an unusually lively one) was an unspeakable certainty that there was something still unexplained. This sense that had clung to him all day could not be fully explained by his fancy about "looking-glass land." Somehow he had not seen the real story, but some game or masque. And yet people do not get hanged or run through the body for the sake of a charade.

As he sat on the steps of the landing-stage ruminating he grew conscious of the tall, dark streak of a sail coming silently down the shining river, and sprang to his feet with such a back-rush of feeling that he almost wept.

"Flambeau!" he cried, and shook his friend by both hands again and again, much to the astonishment of that sportsman, as he came on shore with his fishing tackle. "Flambeau," he said, "so you're not killed?"

"Killed!" repeated the angler in great astonishment. "And why should I be killed?"

"Oh, because nearly everybody else is," said his companion rather wildly. "Saradine got murdered, and Antonelli wants to be hanged, and his mother's fainted, and I, for one, don't know whether I'm in this world or the next. But, thank God, you're in the same one." And he took the bewildered Flambeau's arm.

As they turned from the landing-stage they came under the eaves of the low bamboo house and looked in through one of the windows, as they had done on their first arrival. They beheld a lamp-lit interior well calculated to arrest their eyes. The table in the long dining-room had been laid for dinner when Saradine's destroyer had fallen like a storm-bolt on the island. And the dinner was now in placid progress, for Mrs. Anthony sat somewhat sullenly at the foot of the table, while at the head of it was Mr. Paul, the *major domo*: eating and drinking of the best, his bleared, bluish eyes standing queerly out of his face, his gaunt countenance inscrutable, but by no means devoid of satisfaction.

With a gesture of powerful impatience, Flambeau rattled at the window, wrenched it open, and put an indignant head into the lamp-lit room.

"Well!" he cried; "I can understand you may need some refreshment, but really to steal your master's dinner while he lies murdered in the garden——"

"I have stolen a great many things in a long and pleasant life," replied the strange old gentleman placidly; "this dinner is one of the few things I have not stolen. This dinner and this house and garden happen to belong to me."

A thought flashed across Flambeau's face. "You mean to say," he began, "that the will of Prince Saradine——"

"I am Prince Saradine," said the old man, munching a salted almond.

Father Brown, who was looking at the birds outside, jumped as if he were shot, and put in at the window a pale face like a turnip.

"You are *what*?" he repeated in a shrill voice.

"Paul Prince Saradine, *à vos ordres*," said the venerable person politely, lifting a glass of sherry. "I live here very quietly, being a domestic kind of fellow; and for the sake of modesty I am called Mr. Paul, to distinguish me from my unfortunate brother Mr. Stephen. He died, I hear, recently—in the garden. Of course, it is not my fault if enemies pursue him to this place. It is owing to the regrettable irregularity of his life. He was not a domestic character."

He relapsed into silence, and continued to gaze at the opposite wall just above the bowed and sombre head of the woman. They saw plainly the family likeness that had haunted them in the dead man. Then his old shoulders began to heave and shake a little, as if he were choking, but his face did not alter.

"My God!" cried Flambeau after a pause; "he's laughing!"

"Come away," said Father Brown, who was quite white. "Come away from this house of hell. Let us get into an honest boat again."

Night had sunk on rushes and river by the time they had pushed off from the island, and they went down-stream in the dark, warming themselves with two big cigars that glowed like crimson ships' lanterns. Father Brown took his cigar out of his mouth and said:

"I suppose you can guess the whole story now? After all, it's a primitive story. A man had two enemies. He was a wise man. And so he discovered that two enemies are better than one."

"I do not follow that," answered Flambeau.

"Oh, it's really simple," rejoined his friend. "Simple, though anything but innocent. Both the Saradines were scamps: but the prince, the elder, was the sort of scamp that gets to the top; and the younger, the captain, was the sort that sinks to the bottom. This squalid officer fell from beggar to blackmailer, and one ugly day he got his hold upon his brother the prince. Obviously it was for no light matter, for Prince Paul Saradine was frankly 'fast,' and had no reputation to lose as to the mere sins of society. In plain fact, it was a hanging matter, and Stephen literally had a rope round his brother's neck. He had somehow discovered the truth about the Sicilian affair, and could prove that Paul murdered old Antonelli in the mountains. The captain raked in the hush money heavily for ten years, until even the prince's splendid fortune began to look a little foolish.

"But Prince Saradine bore another burden besides his blood-sucking brother. He knew that the son of Antonelli, a mere child at the time of the murder, had been trained in savage Sicilian loyalty, and lived only to avenge his father, not with the gibbet (for he lacked Stephen's legal proof), but with the old weapons of vendetta. The boy had practised arms with a deadly perfection, and about the time that he was old enough to use them Prince Saradine began, as the society papers said, to travel. The fact is that he began to flee for his life, passing from place to place like a hunted criminal; but with one relentless man upon his trail. That was Prince Paul's position, and by no means a pretty one. The more money he spent on eluding Antonelli the less he had to silence Stephen. The more he gave to silence Stephen the less chance there was of finally escaping Antonelli. Then it was that he showed himself a great man—a genius like Napoleon.

"Instead of resisting his two antagonists, he surrendered suddenly to both of them. He gave way, like a Japanese wrestler, and his foes fell prostrate before him. He gave up the race round the world, and he gave up his address to young Antonelli; then he gave up everything to his brother. He sent Stephen money enough for smart clothes and easy travel, with a letter saying roughly: 'This is all I have left. You have cleaned me out. I still have a little house in Norfolk, with servants and a cellar, and if you want more from me you must take that. Come and take possession if you like, and I will live there quietly as your friend or agent or anything.' He knew that the Sicilian had never seen the Saradine brothers save, perhaps, in pictures; he knew they were somewhat alike, both having grey, pointed beards. Then he shaved his own face and waited. The trap worked. The unhappy captain, in his new clothes, entered the house in triumph as a prince, and walked upon the Sicilian's sword.

"There was one hitch, and it is to the honour of human nature. Evil spirits like Saradine often blunder by never expecting the virtues of mankind. He took it for granted that the Italian's blow, when it came, would be dark, violent and nameless, like the blow it avenged; that the victim would be knifed at night, or shot from behind a hedge, and so die without speech. It was a bad minute for Prince Paul when Antonelli's chivalry proposed a formal duel, with all its possible explanations. It was then that I found him putting off in his boat with wild eyes. He was fleeing, bareheaded, in an open boat before Antonelli should learn who he was.

"But, however agitated, he was not hopeless. He knew the adventurer and he knew the fanatic. It was quite probable that Stephen, the adventurer, would hold his tongue, through his mere histrionic pleasure in playing a part, his lust for clinging to his new cosy quarters, his rascal's trust in luck, and his fine fencing. It was certain that Antonelli, the fanatic, would hold his tongue, and be hanged without telling tales of his family. Paul hung about on the river till he knew the fight was over. Then he roused the town, brought police, saw his two vanquished enemies taken away for ever, and sat down smiling to his dinner."

"Laughing, God help us!" said Flambeau with a strong shudder. "Do they get such ideas from Satan?"

"He's got that idea from you," answered the priest.

"God forbid!" ejaculated Flambeau. "From me? What do you mean?"

The priest pulled a visiting-card from his pocket and held it up in the faint glow of his cigar; it was scrawled with green ink.

"Don't you remember his original invitation to you?" he asked; "and the compliment to your criminal exploit? 'That trick of yours,' he says, 'of getting one detective to arrest the other?' He has just copied your trick. With an enemy on each side of him he slipped swiftly out of the way and let them collide and kill each other."

Flambeau tore Prince Saradine's card from the priest's hands and rent it savagely in small pieces.

"There's the last of that old skull and crossbones," he said as he scattered the pieces upon the dark and disappearing waves of the stream; "but I should think it would poison the fishes."

The last gleam of white card and green ink was drowned and darkened; a faint and vibrant colour as of morning changed the sky, and the moon behind the grasses grew paler. They drifted in silence.

"Father," said Flambeau suddenly, "do you think it was all a dream?"

The priest shook his head, whether in dissent or agnosticism, but remained mute. A smell of hawthorn and of orchards came to them through the darkness, telling them that a wind was awake; the next moment it swayed their little boat and swelled their sail, and carried them onward down the winding river to happier places and the homes of harmless men.

The Sign of the Broken Sword

THE THOUSAND ARMS of the forest were grey, and its million fingers silver. In a sky of dark green-blue-like slate the stars were bleak and brilliant like splintered ice. All that thickly wooded and sparsely tenanted countryside was stiff with a bitter and brittle frost. The black hollows between the trunks of the trees looked like bottomless, black caverns of that heartless Scandinavian hell, a hell of incalculable cold. Even the square stone tower of the church looked northern to the point of heathenry, as if it were some barbaric tower among the sea rocks of Iceland. It was a queer night for anyone to explore a churchyard. But, on the other hand, perhaps it was worth exploring.

It rose abruptly out of the ashen wastes of forest in a sort of hump or shoulder of green turf that looked grey in the starlight. Most of the graves were on a slant, and the path leading up to the church was as steep as a staircase. On the top of the hill, in the one flat and prominent place, was the monument for which the place was famous. It contrasted strangely with the featureless graves all round, for it was the work of one of the greatest sculptors of modern Europe; and yet his fame was at once forgotten in the fame of the man whose image he had made. It showed, by touches of the small silver pencil of starlight, the massive metal figure of a soldier recumbent, the strong hands sealed in an everlasting worship, the great head pillowed upon a gun. The venerable face was bearded, or rather whiskered, in the old, heavy Colonel Newcome fashion. The uniform, though suggested with the few strokes of simplicity, was that of modern war. By his right side lay a sword, of which the tip was broken off; on the left side lay a Bible. On glowing summer afternoons wagonettes came full of Americans and cultured suburbans to see the sepulchre; but even then they felt the vast forest land with its one dumpy dome of churchyard and church as a place oddly dumb and neglected. In this freezing darkness of mid-winter one would think he might be left alone with the stars. Nevertheless, in the stillness of those stiff woods a wooden gate creaked, and two dim figures dressed in black climbed up the little path to the tomb.

So faint was that frigid starlight that nothing could have been traced about them except that while they both wore black, one man was enormously big, and the other (perhaps by contrast) almost startlingly small. They went up to the great graven tomb of the historic warrior, and stood for a few minutes staring at it. There was no human, perhaps no living, thing for a wide circle; and a morbid fancy might well have wondered if they were human themselves. In any case, the beginning of their conversation might have seemed strange. After the first silence the small man said to the other:

"Where does a wise man hide a pebble?"

And the tall man answered in a low voice: "On the beach."

The small man nodded, and after a short silence said: "Where does a wise man hide a leaf?"

And the other answered: "In the forest."

There was another stillness, and then the tall man resumed: "Do you mean that when a wise man has to hide a real diamond he has been known to hide it among sham ones?"

"No, no," said the little man with a laugh, "we will let bygones be bygones."

He stamped his cold feet for a second or two and then said: "I'm not thinking of that at all, but of something else; something rather peculiar. Just strike a match, will you?"

The big man fumbled in his pocket, and soon a scratch and a flare painted gold the whole flat side of the monument. On it was cut in black letters the well-known words which so many Americans had reverently read: "Sacred to the Memory of General Sir Arthur St. Clare, Hero and Martyr, who Always Vanquished his Enemies and Always Spared Them, and Was Treacherously Slain by Them at Last. May God in Whom he Trusted both Reward and Revenge him."

The match burnt the big man's fingers, blackened, and dropped. He was about to strike another, but his small companion stopped him. "That's all right, Flambeau, old man; I saw what I wanted. Or, rather, I didn't see what I didn't want. And now we must walk a mile and a half along the road to the next inn, and I will try to tell you all about it. For Heaven knows a man should have fire and ale when he dares tell such a story."

They descended the precipitous path, they re-latched the rusty gate, and set off at a stamping, ringing walk down the frozen forest road. They had gone a full quarter of a mile before the smaller man spoke again. He said: "Yes; the wise man hides a pebble on the beach. But what does he do if there is no beach? Do you know anything of the great St. Clare trouble?"

"I know nothing about English generals, Father Brown," answered the large man, laughing, "though a little about English policemen. I only know that you have dragged me a precious long dance to all the shrines of this fellow, whoever he is. One would think he got buried in six different places. I've seen a memorial to General St. Clare in Westminster Abbey; I've seen a ramping equestrian statue of General St. Clare on the Embankment; I've seen a medallion of General St. Clare in the street he was born in; and another in the street he lived in; and now you drag me after dark to his coffin in the village churchyard. I am beginning to be a bit tired of his magnificent personality, especially as I don't in the least know who he was. What are you hunting for in all these crypts and effigies?"

"I am only looking for one word," said Father Brown. "A word that isn't there."

"Well," asked Flambeau, "are you going to tell me anything about it?"

"I must divide it into two parts," remarked the priest. "First there is what everybody knows; and then there is what I know. Now, what everybody knows is short and plain enough. It is also entirely wrong."

"Right you are," said the big man called Flambeau cheerfully. "Let's begin at the wrong end. Let's begin with what everybody knows, which isn't true."

"If not wholly untrue, it is at least very inadequate," continued Brown; "for in point of fact, all that the public knows amounts precisely to this: The public knows that Arthur St. Clare was a great and successful English general. It knows that after splendid yet careful campaigns both in India and Africa he was in command against Brazil when the great Brazilian patriot Olivier issued his ultimatum. It knows that on that occasion St. Clare with a very small force attacked Olivier with a very large one, and was captured after heroic resistance. And it knows that after his capture, and to the abhorrence of the civilized world, St. Clare was hanged on the nearest tree. He was found swinging there after the Brazilians had retired, with his broken sword hung round his neck."

"And that popular story is untrue?" suggested Flambeau.

"No," said his friend quietly; "that story is quite true, so far as it goes."

"Well, I think it goes far enough!" said Flambeau, "but if the popular story is true, what is the mystery?"

They had passed many hundreds of grey and ghostly trees before the little priest answered. Then he bit his finger reflectively and said: "Why, the mystery is a mystery of psychology. Or, rather, it is a mystery of two psychologies. In that Brazilian business two of the most famous men of modern history acted flat against their characters. Mind you, Olivier and St. Clare were both heroes—the old thing, and no mistake; it was like the fight between Hector and Achilles. Now, what would you say to an affair in which Achilles was timid and Hector was treacherous?"

"Go on," said the large man impatiently as the other bit his finger again.

"Sir Arthur St. Clare was a soldier of the old religious type—the type that saved us during the Mutiny," continued Brown. "He was always more for duty than for dash; and with all his personal courage was decidedly a prudent commander, particularly indignant at any needless waste of soldiers. Yet, in this last battle, he attempted something that a baby could see was absurd. One need not be a strategist to see it was as wild as wind; just as one need not be a strategist to keep out of the way of a motor-bus. Well, that is the first mystery; what had become of the English general's head? The second riddle is, what had become of the Brazilian general's heart? President Olivier might be called a visionary or a nuisance; but even his enemies admitted that he was magnanimous to the point of knight errantry. Almost every other prisoner he had ever captured had been set free, or even loaded with benefits. Men who had really wronged him came away touched by his simplicity and sweetness. Why the deuce should he diabolically revenge himself only once in his life; and then for the one particular blow that could not have hurt him? Well, there you have it. One of the wisest men in the world acted like an idiot for no reason. One of the best men in the world acted like a fiend for no reason. That's the long and short of it; and I leave it to you, my boy."

"No, you don't," said the other with a snort. "I leave it to you; and you jolly well tell me all about it."

"Well," resumed Father Brown, "it's not fair to say that the public impression is just what I've said, without adding that two things have happened since. I can't say they threw a new light, for nobody can make sense of them. But they threw a new kind of darkness, they threw the darkness in new directions. The first was this. The family physician of the St. Clares quarrelled with that family and began publishing a violent series of articles, in which he said that the late general was a religious maniac; but as far as the tale went, this seemed to mean little more than a religious man. Anyhow, the story fizzled out. Everyone knew, of course, that St. Clare had some of the eccentricities of puritan piety. The second incident was much more arresting. In the luckless and unsupported regiment which made that rash attempt at the Black River there was a certain Captain Keith, who was at that time engaged to St. Clare's daughter, and who afterwards married her. He was one of those who were captured by Olivier, and, like all the rest except the general, appears to have been bounteously treated and promptly set free. Some twenty years afterwards this man, then Lieutenant-Colonel Keith, published a sort of autobiography called 'A British Officer in Burmah and Brazil.' In the place where the reader looks eagerly for some account of the mystery of St. Clare's disaster may be found the following words: 'Everywhere else in this book I have narrated things exactly as they occurred, holding as I do the old-fashioned opinion that the glory of England is old enough to take care of itself. The exception I shall make is in this matter of the defeat by the Black River; and my reasons, though private, are honourable and compelling. I will, however, add this in justice to the memories of two distinguished men. General St. Clare has been accused of incapacity on this occasion; I can at least testify that this action, properly understood, was one of the most brilliant and sagacious of his life. President Olivier by similar report is charged with savage injustice. I think it due to the honour of an enemy to say that he acted on this occasion with even more than his characteristic good feeling. To put the matter popularly, I can assure my countrymen that St. Clare was by no means such a fool, nor Olivier such a brute as he looked. This is all I have to say; nor shall any earthly consideration induce me to add a word.' "

A large frozen moon like a lustrous snowball began to show through the tangle of twigs in front of them, and by its light the narrator had been able to refresh his memory of Captain Keith's text from a scrap of printed paper. As he folded it up and put it back in his pocket Flambeau threw up his hand with a French gesture.

"Wait a bit, wait a bit," he cried excitedly. "I believe I can guess it at the first go."

He strode on, breathing hard, his black head and bull neck forward, like a man winning a walking race. The little priest, amused and interested, had some trouble in trotting beside him. Just before them the trees fell back a little to left and right, and the road swept downwards across a clear, moonlit valley, till it dived again like a rabbit into the wall of another wood. The entrance to the farther forest looked small and round, like the black hole of a remote railway tunnel. But it was within some hundred yards, and gaped like a cavern before Flambeau spoke again.

"I've got it," he cried at last, slapping his thigh with his great hand. "Four minutes' thinking, and I can tell you the whole story myself."

"All right," assented his friend. "You tell it."

Flambeau lifted his head, but lowered his voice. "General Sir Arthur St. Clare," he said, "came of a family in which madness was hereditary; and his whole aim was to keep this from his daughter, and even, if possible, from his future son-in-law. Rightly or wrongly, he thought the final collapse was close, and resolved on suicide. Yet ordinary suicide would blazon the very idea he dreaded. As the campaign approached the clouds came thicker on his brain, and at last in a mad moment he sacrificed his public duty to his private. He rushed rashly into battle, hoping to fall by the first shot. When he found that he had only attained capture and discredit, the sealed bomb in his brain burst, and he broke his own sword and hanged himself."

He stared firmly at the grey façade of forest in front of him, with the one black gap in it, like the mouth of the grave, into which their path plunged. Perhaps something menacing in the road thus suddenly swallowed reinforced his vivid vision of the tragedy, for he shuddered.

"A horrid story," repeated the priest with bent head; "but not the real story."

Then he threw back his head with a sort of despair and cried: "Oh, I wish it had been."

The tall Flambeau faced round and stared at him.

"Yours is a clean story," cried Father Brown, deeply moved. "A sweet, pure, honest story, as open and white as that moon. Madness and despair are innocent enough. There are worse things, Flambeau."

Flambeau looked up wildly at the moon thus invoked; and from where he stood one black tree-bough curved across it exactly like a devil's horn.

"Father—Father," cried Flambeau with the French gesture and stepping yet more rapidly forward, "do you mean it was worse than that?"

"Worse than that," said the other like a grave echo. And they plunged into the black cloister of the woodland, which ran by them in a dim tapestry of trunks, like one of the dark corridors in a dream.

They were soon in the most secret entrails of the wood, and felt close about them the foliage that they could not see, when the priest said again:

"Where does a wise man hide a leaf? In the forest. But what does he do if there is no forest?"

"Well—well," cried Flambeau irritably, "what does he do?"

"He grows a forest to hide it in," said the priest in an obscure voice. "A fearful sin."

"Look here," cried his friend impatiently, for the dark wood and the dark sayings got a little on his nerves; "will you tell me this story or not? What other evidence is there to go on?"

"There are three more bits of evidence," said the other, "that I have dug up in holes and corners, and I will give them in logical rather than chronological order. First of all, of course, our authority for the issue and event of the battle is in Olivier's own dispatches, which are lucid enough. He was entrenched with two or three regiments on the heights that swept down to the Black River, on the other side of which was lower and more marshy ground. Beyond this again was gently rising country, on which was the first English outpost, supported by others which lay, however, considerably in its rear. The British forces as a whole were greatly superior in numbers; but this particular regiment was just far enough from its base to make Olivier consider the project of crossing the river to cut it off. By sunset, however, he had decided to retain his own position, which was a specially strong one. At daybreak next morning he was thunderstruck to see that this stray handful of English, entirely unsupported from their rear, had flung themselves across the river, half by the bridge to the right, and the other half by a ford higher up, and were massed upon the marshy bank below him.

"That they should attempt an attack with such numbers against such a position was incredible enough; but Olivier noticed something yet more extraordinary. For instead of attempting to seize more solid ground, this mad regiment, having put the river in its rear by one wild charge, did nothing more, but stuck there in the mire like flies in treacle. Needless to say, the Brazilians blew great gaps in them with artillery, which they could only return with spirited but lessening rifle fire. Yet they never broke; and Olivier's curt account ends with a strong tribute of admiration for the mystic valour of these imbeciles. 'Our line then advanced finally,' writes Olivier, 'and drove them into the river; we captured General St. Clare himself and several other officers. The colonel and the major had both fallen in the battle. I cannot resist saying that few finer sights can have been seen in history than the last stand of this extraordinary regiment; wounded officers picking up the rifles of dead soldiers, and the general himself facing us on horseback bare-headed and with a broken sword.' On what happened to the general afterwards Olivier is as silent as Captain Keith."

"Well," grunted Flambeau, "get on to the next bit of evidence."

"The next evidence," said Father Brown, "took some time to find, but it will not take long to tell. I found at last, in an almshouse down in the Lincolnshire Fens, an old soldier who not only was wounded at the Black River, but had actually knelt beside the colonel of the regiment when he died. This latter was a certain Colonel Clancy, a big bull of an Irishman; and it would seem that he died almost as much of rage as of bullets. He, at any rate, was not responsible for that ridiculous raid; it must have been imposed on him by the general. His last edifying words, according to my informant, were these: 'And there goes the damned old donkey with the end of his sword knocked off. I wish it was his head.' You will remark that everyone seems to have noticed this detail about the broken sword blade, though most people regard it somewhat more reverently than did the late Colonel Clancy. And now for the third fragment."

Their path through the woodland began to go upward, and the speaker paused a little for breath before he went on. Then he continued in the same business-like tone:

"Only a month or two ago a certain Brazilian official died in England, having quarrelled with Olivier and left his country. He was a well-known figure both here and on the Continent, a Spaniard named Espado; I knew him myself, a yellow-faced old dandy, with a hooked nose. For various private reasons I had permission to see the documents he had left; he was a Catholic, of course, and I had been with him towards the end. There was nothing of his that lit up any corner of the black St. Clare business, except five or six common exercise books filled with the diary of some English soldier. I can only suppose that it was found by the Brazilians on one of those that fell. Anyhow, it stopped abruptly the night before the battle.

"But the account of that last day in the poor fellow's life was certainly worth reading. I have it on me; but it's too dark to read it here, and I will give you a résumé. The first part of that entry is full of jokes, evidently flung about among the men, about somebody called the Vulture. It does not seem as if this person, whoever he was, was one of themselves, nor even an Englishman; neither is he exactly spoken of as one of the enemy. It sounds rather as if he were some local go-between and non-combatant; perhaps a guide or a journalist. He has been closeted with old Colonel Clancy; but is more often seen talking to the major. Indeed, the major is somewhat prominent in this soldier's narrative; a lean, dark-haired man, apparently, of the name of Murray—a north of Ireland man and a Puritan. There are continual jests about the contrast between this Ulsterman's austerity and the conviviality of Colonel Clancy. There is also some joke about the Vulture wearing bright-coloured clothes.

"But all these levities are scattered by what may well be called the note of a bugle. Behind the English camp, and almost parallel to the river, ran one of the few great roads of that district. Westward the road curved round towards the river, which it crossed by the bridge before mentioned. To the east the road swept backwards into the wilds, and some two miles along it was the next English outpost. From this direction there came along the road that evening a glitter and clatter of light cavalry, in which even the simple diarist could recognize with astonishment the general with his staff. He rode the great white horse which you have seen so often in illustrated papers and Academy pictures; and you may be sure that the salute they gave him was not merely ceremonial. He, at least, wasted no time on ceremony, but, springing from the saddle immediately, mixed with the group of officers, and fell into emphatic though confidential speech. What struck our friend the diarist most was his special disposition to discuss matters with Major Murray; but, indeed, such a selection, so long as it was not marked, was in no way unnatural. The two men were made for sympathy; they were men who 'read their Bibles'; they were both the old Evangelical type of officer. However this may be, it is certain that when the general mounted again he was still talking earnestly to Murray; and that as he walked his horse slowly down the road towards the river, the tall Ulsterman still walked by his bridle-rein in earnest debate. The soldiers watched the two until they vanished behind a clump of trees where the road turned towards the river. The colonel had gone back to his tent, and the men to their pickets; the man with the diary lingered for another four minutes, and saw a marvellous sight.

"The great white horse which had marched slowly down the road, as it had marched in so many processions, flew back, galloping up the road towards them as if it were mad to win a race. At first they thought it had run away with the man on its back; but they soon saw that the general, a fine rider, was himself urging it to full speed. Horse and man swept up to them like a whirlwind; and then, reining up the reeling charger, the general turned on them a face like flame, and called for the colonel like the trumpet that wakes the dead.

"I conceive that all the earthquake events of that catastrophe tumbled on top of each other rather like lumber in the minds of men such as our friend with the diary. With the dazed excitement of a dream, they found themselves falling—literally falling—into their ranks, and learned that an attack was to be led at once across the river. The general and the major, it was said, had found out something at the bridge, and there was only just time to strike for life. The major had gone back at once to call up the reserve along the road behind; it was doubtful if even with that prompt appeal help could reach them in time. But they must pass the stream that night, and seize the heights by morning. It is with the very stir and throb of that romantic nocturnal march that the diary suddenly ends."

Father Brown had mounted ahead; for the woodland path grew smaller, steeper, and more twisted, till they felt as if they were ascending a winding staircase. The priest's voice came from above out of the darkness.

"There was one other little and enormous thing. When the general urged them to their chivalric charge he drew half his sword from the scabbard; and then, as if ashamed of such melodrama, thrust it back again. The sword again, you see."

A half-light broke through the network of boughs above them, flinging the ghost of a net about their feet; for they were mounting again to the faint luminosity of the naked night. Flambeau felt truth·all round him as an atmosphere, but not as an idea. He answered with bewildered brain: "Well, what's the matter with the sword? Officers generally have swords, don't they?"

"They are not often mentioned in modern war," said the other dispassionately; "but in this affair one falls over the blessed sword everywhere."

"Well, what is there in that?" growled Flambeau; "it was a twopence coloured sort of incident; the old man's blade breaking in his last battle. Anyone might bet the papers would get hold of it, as they have. On all these tombs and things it's shown broken at the point. I hope you haven't dragged me through this Polar expedition merely because two men with an eye for a picture saw St. Clare's broken sword."

"No," cried Father Brown, with a sharp voice like a pistol shot; "but who saw his unbroken sword?"

"What do you mean?" cried the other, and stood still under the stars. They had come abruptly out of the grey gates of the wood.

"I say, who saw his unbroken sword?" repeated Father Brown obstinately. "Not the writer of the diary, anyhow; the general sheathed it in time."

Flambeau looked about him in the moonlight, as a man struck blind might look in the sun; and his friend went on for the first time with eagerness:

"Flambeau," he cried, "I cannot prove it, even after hunting through the tombs. But I am sure of it. Let me add just one more tiny fact that tips the whole thing over. The colonel, by a strange chance, was one of the first struck by a bullet. He was struck long before the troops came to close quarters. But he saw St. Clare's sword broken. Why was it broken? How was it broken? My friend, it was broken before the battle."

"Oh!" said his friend, with a sort of forlorn jocularity; "and pray where is the other piece?"

"I can tell you," said the priest promptly. "In the north-east corner of the cemetery of the Protestant Cathedral at Belfast."

"Indeed?" inquired the other. "Have you looked for it?"

"I couldn't," replied Brown, with frank regret. "There's a great marble monument on top of it; a monument to the heroic Major Murray, who fell fighting gloriously at the famous Battle of the Black River."

Flambeau seemed suddenly galvanized into existence. "You mean," he cried hoarsely, "that General St. Clare hated Murray, and murdered him on the field of battle because——"

"You are still full of good and pure thoughts," said the other. "It was worse than that."

"Well," said the large man, "my stock of evil imagination is used up."

The priest seemed really doubtful where to begin, and at last he said again:

"Where would a wise man hide a leaf? In the forest."

The other did not answer.

"If there were no forest, he would make a forest. And if he wished to hide a dead leaf, he would make a dead forest."

There was still no reply, and the priest added still more mildly and quietly:

"And if a man had to hide a dead body, he would make a field of dead bodies to hide it in."

Flambeau began to stamp forward with an intolerance of delay in time or space; but Father Brown went on as if he were continuing the last sentence:

"Sir Arthur St. Clare, as I have already said, was a man who read his Bible. That was what was the matter with *him*. When will people understand that it is useless for a man to read his Bible unless he also reads everybody else's Bible? A printer reads a Bible for misprints. A Mormon reads his Bible and finds polygamy; a Christian Scientist reads his and finds we have no arms and legs. St. Clare was an old Anglo-Indian Protestant soldier. Now, just think what that might mean; and, for Heaven's sake, don't cant about it. It might mean a man physically formidable living under a tropic sun in an Oriental society, and soaking himself without sense or guidance in an Oriental book. Of course, he read the Old Testament rather than the New. Of course, he found in the Old Testament anything that he wanted—lust, tyranny, treason. Oh, I dare say he was honest, as you call it. But what is the good of a man being honest in his worship of dishonesty?

"In each of the hot and secret countries to which that man went he kept a harem, he tortured witnesses, he amassed shameful gold; but certainly he would have said with steady eyes that he did it to the glory of the Lord. My own theology is sufficiently expressed by asking which Lord? Anyhow, there is this about such evil, that it opens door after door in hell, and always into smaller and smaller chambers. This is the real case against crime, that a man does not become wilder and wilder, but only meaner and meaner. St. Clare was soon suffocated by difficulties of bribery and blackmail; and needed more and more cash. And by the time of the battle of the Black River he had fallen from world to world to that place which Dante makes the lowest floor of the universe."

"What do you mean?" asked his friend again.

"I mean *that*," retorted the cleric, and suddenly pointed at a puddle sealed with ice that shone in the moon. "Do you remember whom Dante put in the last circle of ice?"

"The traitors," said Flambeau, and shuddered. As he looked round at the inhuman landscape of trees, with taunting and almost obscene outlines, he could almost fancy he was Dante, and the priest with the rivulet of a voice was, indeed, a Virgil leading him through a land of eternal sins.

The voice went on: "Olivier, as you know, was quixotic, and would not permit a secret service and spies. The thing, however, was done, like many other things, behind his back. It was managed by my old friend Espado; he was the bright-clad fop, whose hook nose got him called the Vulture. Posing as a sort of philanthropist at the front, he felt his way through the English Army, and at last got his fingers on its one corrupt man—please God!—and that man at the top. St. Clare was in foul need of money, and mountains of it. The discredited family doctor was threatening those extraordinary exposures that afterwards began and were broken off; tales of monstrous and prehistoric things in Park Lane; things done by an English Evangelical that smelt like human sacrifice and hordes of slaves. Money was wanted, too, for his daughter's dowry; for to him the fame of wealth was as sweet as wealth itself. He snapped the last thread, whispered the word to Brazil, and wealth poured in from the enemies of England. But another man had talked to Espado the Vulture as well as he. Somehow the dark, grim young major from Ulster had guessed the hideous truth; and when they walked slowly together down that road towards the bridge Murray was telling the general that he must resign instantly, or be court-martialled and shot. The general temporized with him till they came to the fringe of tropic trees by the bridge; and there by the singing river and the sunlit palms (for I can see the picture) the general drew his sabre and plunged it through the body of the major."

The wintry road curved over a ridge in cutting frost, with cruel black shapes of bush and thicket; but Flambeau fancied that he saw beyond it faintly the edge of an aureole that was not starlight and moonlight, but some fire such as is made by men. He watched it as the tale drew to its close.

"St. Clare was a hell-hound, but he was a hound of breed. Never, I'll swear, was he so lucid and so strong as when poor Murray lay a cold lump at his feet. Never in all his triumphs, as Captain Keith said truly, was the great man so great as he was in this last world-despised defeat. He looked coolly at his weapon to wipe off the blood; he saw the point he had planted between his victim's shoulders had broken off in the body. He saw quite calmly as, through a club window-pane, all that must follow. He saw that men must find the unaccountable corpse; must extract the unaccountable sword-point; must notice the unaccountable broken sword—or absence of sword. He had killed, but not silenced. But his imperious intellect rose against the facer—there was one way yet. He could make the corpse less unaccountable. He could create a hill of corpses to cover this one. In twenty minutes eight hundred English soldiers were marching down to their death."

The warmer glow behind the black winter wood grew richer and brighter, and Flambeau strode on to reach it. Father Brown also quickened his stride; but he seemed merely absorbed in his tale.

"Such was the valour of that English thousand, and such the genius of their commander, that if they had at once attacked the hill, even their mad march might have met some luck. But the evil mind that played with them like pawns had other aims and reasons. They must remain in the marshes by the bridge at least till British corpses should be a common sight there. Then for the last grand scene: the silver-haired soldier-saint would give up his shattered sword to save further slaughter. Oh, it was well organized for an impromptu. But I think (I cannot prove), I think that it was while they stuck there in the bloody mire that someone doubted—and someone guessed."

He was mute a moment, and then said: "There is a voice from nowhere that tells me the man who guessed was the lover . . . the man to wed the old man's child."

"But what about Olivier and the hanging?" asked Flambeau.

"Olivier, partly from chivalry, partly from policy, seldom encumbered his march with captives," explained the narrator. "He released everybody in most cases. He released everybody in this case."

"Everybody but the general," said the tall man.

"Everybody," said the priest.

Flambeau knitted his black brows. "I don't grasp it all yet," he said.

"There is another picture, Flambeau," said Brown in his more mystical undertone. "I can't prove it; but I can do more—I can see it. There is a camp breaking up on the bare, torrid hills at morning, and Brazilian uniforms massed in blocks and columns to march. There is the red shirt and long black beard of Olivier, which blows as he stands, his broad-brimmed hat in his hand. He is saying farewell to the great enemy he is setting free—the simple, snow-headed English veteran, who thanks him in the name of his men. The English remnant stand behind at attention; beside them are stores and vehicles for the retreat. The drums roll; the Brazilians are moving; the English are still like statues. So they abide till the last hum and flash of the enemy have faded from the tropic horizon. Then they alter their postures all at once, like dead men coming to life; they turn their fifty faces upon the general—faces not to be forgotten."

Flambeau gave a great jump. "Ah," he cried. "You don't mean——"

"Yes," said Father Brown in a deep, moving voice. "It was an English hand that put the rope around St. Clare's neck; I believe the hand that put the ring on his daughter's finger. They were English hands that dragged him up to the tree of shame; the hands of men that had adored him and followed him to victory. And they were English souls (God pardon and endure us all!) who stared at him swinging in that foreign sun on the green gallows of palm, and prayed in their hatred that he might drop off it into hell."

As the two topped the ridge there burst on them the strong scarlet light of a red-curtained English inn. It stood sideways in the road, as if standing aside in the amplitude of hospitality. Its three doors stood open with invitation; and even where they stood they could hear the hum and laughter of humanity happy for a night.

"I need not tell you more," said Father Brown. "They tried him in the wilderness and destroyed him; and then, for the honour of England and of his daughter, they took an oath to seal up for ever the story of the traitor's purse and the assassin's sword blade. Perhaps—Heaven help them—they tried to forget it. Let us try to forget it, anyhow; here is our inn."

"With all my heart," said Flambeau, and was just striding into the bright, noisy bar when he stepped back and almost fell on the road.

"Look there, in the devil's name!" he cried, and pointed rigidly at the square wooden sign that overhung the road. It showed dimly the crude shape of a sabre hilt and a shortened blade; and was inscribed in false archaic lettering, "The Sign of the Broken Sword."

"Were you not prepared?" asked Father Brown gently. "He is the god of this country; half the inns and parks and streets are named after him and his story."

"I thought we had done with the leper," cried Flambeau, and spat on the road.

"You will never have done with him in England," said the priest, looking down, "while brass is strong and stone abides. His marble statues will erect the souls of proud, innocent boys for centuries, his village tomb will smell of loyalty as of lilies. Millions who never knew him shall love him like a father—this man whom the last few that knew him dealt with like dung. He shall be a saint; and the truth shall never be told of him, because I have made up my mind at last. There is so much good and evil in breaking secrets, that I put my conduct to a test. All these newspapers will perish; the anti-Brazil boom is already over; Olivier is already honoured everywhere. But I told myself that if anywhere, by name, in metal or marble that will endure like the pyramids, Colonel Clancy, or Captain Keith, or President Olivier, or any innocent man was wrongly blamed, then I would speak. If it were only that St. Clare was wrongly praised, I would be silent. And I will."

They plunged into the red-curtained tavern, which was not only cosy, but even luxurious inside. On a table stood a silver model of the tomb of St. Clare, the silver head bowed, the silver sword broken. On the walls were coloured photographs of the same scene, and of the system of wagonettes that took tourists to see it. They sat down on the comfortable padded benches.

"Come, it's cold," cried Father Brown; "let's have some wine or beer."

"Or brandy," said Flambeau.

The Man in the Passage

TWO MEN APPEARED simultaneously at the two ends of a sort of passage running along the side of the Apollo Theatre in the Adelphi. The evening daylight in the streets was large and luminous, opalescent and empty. The passage was comparatively long and dark, so each man could see the other as a mere black silhouette at the other end. Nevertheless, each man knew the other, even in that inky outline, for they were both men of striking appearance, and they hated each other.

The covered passage opened at one end on one of the steep streets of the Adelphi, and at the other on a terrace overlooking the sunset-coloured river. One side of the passage was a blank wall, for the building it supported was an old unsuccessful theatre restaurant, now shut up. The other side of the passage contained two doors, one at each end. Neither was what was commonly called the stage door; they were a sort of special and private stage doors, used by very special performers, and in this case by the star actor and actress in the Shakespearean performance of the day. Persons of that eminence often like to have such private exits and entrances, for meeting friends or avoiding them.

The two men in question were certainly two such friends, men who evidently knew the doors and counted on their opening, for each approached the door at the upper end with equal coolness and confidence. Not, however, with equal speed; but the man who walked fast was the man from the other end of the tunnel, so they both arrived before the secret stage door almost at the same instant. They saluted each other with civility, and waited a moment before one of them, the sharper walker, who seemed to have the shorter patience, knocked at the door.

In this and everything else each man was opposite and neither could be called inferior. As private persons, both were handsome, capable, and popular. As public persons, both were in the first public rank. But everything about them, from their glory to their good looks, was of a diverse and incomparable kind. Sir Wilson Seymour was the kind of man whose importance is known to everybody who knows. The more you mixed with the innermost ring in every polity or profession, the more often you met Sir Wilson Seymour. He was the one intelligent man on twenty unintelligent committees—on every sort of subject, from the reform of the Royal Academy to the project of bimetallism for Greater Britain. In the arts especially he was omnipotent. He was so unique that nobody could quite decide whether he was a great aristocrat who had taken up art, or a great artist whom the aristocrats had taken up. But you could not meet him for five minutes without realising that you had really been ruled by him all your life.

His appearance was "distinguished" in exactly the same sense; it was at once conventional and unique. Fashion could have found no fault with his high silk hat; yet it was unlike anyone else's hat—a little higher, perhaps, and adding something to his natural height. His tall, slender figure had a slight stoop, yet it looked the reverse of feeble. His hair was silver-grey, but he did not look old; it was worn longer than the common, yet he did not look effeminate; it was curly, but it did not look curled. His carefully pointed beard made him look more manly and militant rather than otherwise, as it does in those old admirals of Velasquez with whose dark portraits his house was hung. His grey gloves were a shade bluer, his silver-knobbed cane a shade longer than scores of such gloves and canes flapped and flourished about the theatres and the restaurants.

The other man was not so tall, yet would have struck nobody as short, but merely as strong and handsome. His hair also was curly, but fair and cropped close to a strong, massive head—the sort of head you break a door with, as Chaucer said of the Miller's. His military moustache and the carriage of his shoulders showed him a soldier, but he had a pair of those peculiar, frank, and piercing blue eyes which are more common in sailors. His face was somewhat square, his jaw was square, his shoulders were square, even his jacket was square. Indeed, in the wild school of caricature then current, Mr. Max Beerbohm had represented him as a proposition in the fourth book of Euclid.

For he also was a public man, though with quite another sort of success. You did not have to be in the best society to have heard of Captain Cutler, of the siege of Hong-Kong and the great march across China. You could not get away from hearing of him wherever you were; his portrait was on every other postcard; his maps and battles in every other illustrated paper; songs in his honour in every other music-hall turn or on every other barrel-organ. His fame, though probably more temporary, was ten times more wide, popular, and spontaneous than the other man's. In thousands of English homes he appeared enormous above

England, like Nelson. Yet he had infinitely less power in England than Sir Wilson Seymour.

The door was opened to them by an aged servant or "dresser," whose broken-down face and figure and black shabby coat and trousers contrasted queerly with the glittering interior of the great actress's dressing-room. It was fitted and filled with looking-glasses at every angle of refraction, so that they looked like the hundred facets of one huge diamond—if one could get inside a diamond. The other features of luxury, a few flowers, a few coloured cushions, a few scraps of stage costume, were multiplied by all the mirrors into the madness of the Arabian Nights, and danced and changed places perpetually as the shuffling attendant shifted a mirror outwards or shot one back against the wall.

They both spoke to the dingy dresser by name, calling him Parkinson, and asking for the lady as Miss Aurora Rome. Parkinson said she was in the other room, but he would go and tell her. A shade crossed the brow of both visitors; for the other room was the private room of the great actor with whom Miss Aurora was performing, and she was of the kind that does not inflame admiration without inflaming jealousy. In about half a minute, however, the inner door opened, and she entered as she always did, even in private life, so that the very silence seemed to be a roar of applause, and one well deserved. She was clad in a somewhat strange garb of peacock green and peacock blue satins, that gleamed like blue and green metals, such as delight children and æsthetes, and her heavy, hot brown hair framed one of those magic faces which are dangerous to all men, but especially to boys and to men growing grey. In company with her male colleague, the great American actor, Isidore Bruno, she was producing a particularly poetical and fantastic interpretation of the *Midsummer Night's Dream*, in which the artistic prominence was given to Oberon and Titania, or in other words to Bruno and herself. Set in dreamy and exquisite scenery, and moving in mystical dances, the green costume, like burnished beetle-wings, expressed all the elusive individuality of an elfin queen. But when personally confronted in what was still broad daylight, a man looked only at the woman's face.

She greeted both men with the beaming and baffling smile which kept so many males at the same just dangerous distance from her. She accepted some flowers from Cutler, which were as tropical and expensive as his victories; and another sort of present from Sir Wilson Seymour, offered later on and more nonchalantly by that gentleman. For it was against his breeding to show eagerness, and against his conventional unconventionality to give anything so obvious as flowers. He had picked up a trifle, he said, which was rather a curiosity; it was an ancient Greek dagger of the Mycenean Epoch, and might have been well worn in the time of Theseus and Hippolyta. It was made of brass like all the Heroic weapons, but, oddly enough, sharp enough to prick anyone still. He had really been attracted to it by the leaflike shape; it was as perfect as a Greek vase. If it was of any interest to Miss Rome or could come in anywhere in the play, he hoped she would——

The inner door burst open and a big figure appeared, who was more of a contrast to the explanatory Seymour than even Captain Cutler. Nearly six-foot-six, and of more than theatrical thews and muscles, Isidore Bruno, in the gorgeous leopard skin and golden-brown garments of Oberon, looked like a barbaric god. He leaned on a sort of hunting-spear, which across a theatre looked a slight, silvery wand, but which in the small and comparatively crowded room looked as plain as a pikestaff— and as menacing. His vivid, black eyes rolled volcanically, his bronzed face, handsome as it was, showed at that moment a combination of high cheekbones with set white teeth, which recalled certain American conjectures about his origin in the Southern plantations.

"Aurora," he began, in that deep voice like a drum of passion that had moved so many audiences, "will you——"

He stopped indecisively because a sixth figure had suddenly presented itself just inside the doorway—a figure so incongruous in the scene as to be almost comic. It was a very short man in the black uniform of the Roman secular clergy, and looking (especially in such a presence as Bruno's and Aurora's) rather like the wooden Noah out of an ark. He did not, however, seem conscious of any contrast, but said with dull civility: "I believe Miss Rome sent for me."

A shrewd observer might have remarked that the emotional temperature rather rose at so unemotional an interruption. The detachment of a professional celibate seemed to reveal to the others that they stood round the woman as a ring of amorous rivals; just as a stranger coming in with frost on his coat will reveal that a room is like a furnace. The presence of the one man who did not care about her increased Miss Rome's sense that everybody else was in love with her, and each in a somewhat dangerous way: the actor with all the appetite of a savage and a spoilt child; the soldier with all the simple selfishness of a man of will rather than mind; Sir Wilson with that daily hardening concentration with which old Hedonists take to a hobby; nay, even the abject Parkinson, who had known her before her triumphs, and who followed her about the room with eyes or feet, with the dumb fascination of a dog.

A shrewd person might also have noted a yet odder thing. The man like a black wooden Noah (who was not wholly without shrewdness) noted it with a considerable but contained amusement. It was evident that the great Aurora, though by no means indifferent to the admiration of the other sex, wanted at this moment to get rid of all the men who admired her and be left alone with the man who did not—did not admire her in that sense, at least; for the little priest did admire and even enjoy the firm feminine diplomacy with which she set about her task. There was, perhaps, only one thing that Aurora Rome was clever about, and that was one half of humanity—the other half. The little priest watched, like a Napoleonic campaign, the swift precision of her policy for expelling all while banishing none. Bruno, the big actor, was so babyish that it was easy to send him off in brute sulks, banging the door. Cutler, the British officer, was pachydermatous to ideas, but punctilious about behaviour. He would ignore all hints, but he would die rather than ignore a definite commission from a lady. As to old Seymour he had to be treated differently; he had to be left to the last. The only way to move him was to appeal to him in confidence as an old friend, to let him into the secret of the clearance. The priest did really admire Miss Rome as she achieved all these three objects in one selected action.

She went across to Captain Cutler and said in her sweetest manner: "I shall value all these flowers because they must be your favourite flowers. But they won't be complete, you know, without *my* favourite flower. *Do* go over to that shop round the corner and get me some lilies-of-the-valley and then it will be *quite lovely.*"

The first object of her diplomacy, the exit of the enraged Bruno, was at once achieved. He had already handed his spear in a lordly style like a sceptre to the piteous Parkinson, and was about to assume one of the cushioned seats like a throne. But at this open appeal to his rival there glowed in his opal eyeballs all the sensitive insolence of the slave; he knotted his enormous brown fists for an instant, and then, dashing open the door, disappeared into his own apartments beyond. But meanwhile Miss Rome's experiment in mobilising the British Army had not succeeded so simply as seemed probable. Cutler had indeed risen stiffly and suddenly, and walked towards the door, hatless, as if at a word of command. But perhaps there was something ostentatiously elegant about the languid figure of Seymour leaning against one of the looking-glasses, that brought him up short at the entrance, turning his head this way and that like a bewildered bulldog.

"I must show this stupid man where to go," said Aurora in a whisper to Seymour, and ran out to the threshold to speed the parting guest.

Seymour seemed to be listening, elegant and unconscious as was his posture, and he seemed relieved when he heard the lady call out some last instructions to the Captain, and then turn sharply and run laughing down the passage towards the other end, the end on the terrace above the

Thames. Yet a second or two after, Seymour's brow darkened again. A man in his position has so many rivals, and he remembered that at the other end of the passage was the corresponding entrance to Bruno's private room. He did not lose his dignity; he said some civil words to Father Brown about the revival of Byzantine architecture in the Westminster Cathedral, and then, quite naturally, strolled out himself into the upper end of the passage. Father Brown and Parkinson were left alone, and they were neither of them men with a taste for superfluous conversation. The dresser went round the room, pulling out looking-glasses and pushing them in again, his dingy dark coat and trousers looking all the more dismal since he was still holding the festive fairy spear of King Oberon. Every time he pulled out the frame of a new glass, a new black figure of Father Brown appeared; the absurd glass chamber was full of Father Browns, upside down in the air like angels, turning somersaults like acrobats, turning their backs to everybody like very rude persons.

Father Brown seemed quite unconscious of this cloud of witnesses, but followed Parkinson with an idly attentive eye till he took himself and his absurd spear into the farther room of Bruno. Then he abandoned himself to such abstract meditations as always amused him—calculating the angles of the mirrors, the angles of each refraction, the angle at which each must fit into the wall . . . when he heard a strong but strangled cry.

He sprang to his feet and stood rigidly listening. At the same instant Sir Wilson Seymour burst back into the room, white as ivory. "Who's that man in the passage?" he cried. "Where's that dagger of mine?"

Before Father Brown could turn in his heavy boots, Seymour was plunging about the room looking for the weapon. And before he could possibly find that weapon or any other, a brisk running of feet broke upon the pavement outside, and the square face of Cutler was thrust into the same doorway. He was still grotesquely grasping a bunch of lilies-of-the-valley. "What's this?" he cried. "What's that creature down the passage? Is this some of your tricks?"

"My tricks!" hissed his pale rival, and made a stride towards him.

In the instant of time in which all this happened Father Brown stepped out into the top of the passage, looked down it, and at once walked briskly towards what he saw.

At this the other two men dropped their quarrel and darted after him, Cutler calling out: "What are you doing? Who are you?"

"My name is Brown," said the priest sadly, as he bent over something and straightened himself again. "Miss Rome sent for me, and I came as quickly as I could. I have come too late."

The three men looked down, and in one of them at least the life died in that late light of afternoon. It ran along the passage like a path of gold, and in the midst of it Aurora Rome lay lustrous in her robes of green and gold, with her dead face turned upwards. Her dress was torn away as in a struggle, leaving the right shoulder bare, but the wound from which the blood was welling was on the other side. The brass dagger lay flat and gleaming a yard or so away.

There was a blank stillness for a measurable time; so that they could hear far off a flower-girl's laugh outside Charing Cross, and someone whistling furiously for a taxicab in one of the streets off the Strand. Then the Captain, with a movement so sudden that it might have been passion or play-acting, took Sir Wilson Seymour by the throat.

Seymour looked at him steadily without either fight or fear. "You need not kill me," he said, in a voice quite cold; "I shall do that on my own account."

The Captain's hand hesitated and dropped; and the other added with the same icy candour: "If I find I haven't the nerve to do it with that dagger, I can do it in a month with drink."

"Drink isn't good enough for me," replied Cutler, "but I'll have blood for this before I die. Not yours—but I think I know whose."

And before the others could appreciate his intention he snatched up the dagger, sprang at the other door at the lower end of the passage, burst it open, bolt and all, and confronted Bruno in his dressing-room. As he did so, old Parkinson tottered in his wavering way out of the door and caught sight of the corpse lying in the passage. He moved shakily towards it; looked at it weakly with a working face; then moved shakily back into the dressing-room again, and sat down suddenly on one of the richly cushioned chairs. Father Brown instantly ran across to him, taking no notice of Cutler and the colossal actor, though the room already rang with their blows and they began to struggle for the dagger. Seymour, who retained some practical sense, was whistling for the police at the end of the passage.

When the police arrived it was to tear the two men from an almost apelike grapple; and, after a few formal inquiries, to arrest Isidore Bruno upon a charge of murder, brought against him by his furious opponent. The idea that the great national hero of the hour had arrested a wrong-doer with his own hand doubtless had its weight with the police, who are not without elements of the journalist. They treated Cutler with a certain solemn attention, and pointed out that he had got a slight slash on the hand. Even as Cutler bore him back across tilted chair and table, Bruno had twisted the dagger out of his grasp and disabled him just below the wrist. The injury was really slight, but till he was removed from the room the half-savage prisoner stared at the running blood with a steady smile.

"Looks a cannibal sort of chap, don't he?" said the constable confidentially to Cutler.

Cutler made no answer, but said sharply a moment after: "We must attend to the . . . the death . . ." and his voice escaped from articulation.

"The two deaths," came in the voice of the priest from the farther side of the room. "This poor fellow was gone when I got across to him." And he stood looking down at old Parkinson, who sat in a black huddle on the gorgeous chair. He also had paid his tribute, not without eloquence, to the woman who had died.

The silence was first broken by Cutler, who seemed not untouched by a rough tenderness. "I wish I was him," he said huskily. "I remember he used to watch her wherever she walked more than—anybody. She was his air, and he's dried up. He's just dead."

"We are all dead," said Seymour, in a strange voice, looking down the road.

They took leave of Father Brown at the corner of the road, with some random apologies for any rudeness they might have shown. Both their faces were tragic, but also cryptic.

The mind of the little priest was always a rabbit-warren of wild thoughts that jumped too quickly for him to catch them. Like the white tail of a rabbit, he had the vanishing thought that he was certain of their grief, but not so certain of their innocence.

"We had better all be going," said Seymour heavily; "we have done all we can to help."

"Will you understand my motives," asked Father Brown quietly, "if I say you have done all you can to hurt?"

They both started as if guiltily, and Cutler said sharply: "To hurt whom?"

"To hurt yourselves," answered the priest. "I would not add to your troubles if it weren't common justice to warn you. You've done nearly everything you could do to hang yourselves, if this actor should be acquitted. They'll be sure to subpœna me; I shall be bound to say that after the cry was heard, each of you rushed into the room in a wild state and began quarrelling about a dagger. As far as my words on oath can go, you might either of you have done it. You hurt yourselves with that; and then Captain Cutler must hurt himself with the dagger."

"Hurt myself!" exclaimed the Captain, with contempt. "A silly little scratch."

"Which drew blood," replied the priest, nodding. "We know there's blood on the brass now. And so we shall never know whether there was blood on it before."

There was a silence; and then Seymour said, with an emphasis quite alien to his daily accent: "But I saw a man in the passage."

"I know you did," answered the cleric Brown, with a face of wood; "so did Captain Cutler. That's what seems so improbable."

Before either could make sufficient sense of it even to answer, Father Brown had politely excused himself and gone stumping up the road with his stumpy old umbrella.

As modern newspapers are conducted, the most honest and most important news is the police news. If it be true that in the twentieth century more space was given to murder than to politics, it was for the excellent reason that murder is a more serious subject. But even this would hardly explain the enormous omnipresence and widely distributed detail of "The Bruno Case," or "The Passage Mystery," in the Press of London and the provinces. So vast was the excitement that for some weeks the Press really told the truth; and the reports of examination and cross-examination, if interminable, even if intolerable, are at least reliable. The true reason, of course, was the coincidence of persons. The victim was a popular actress; the accused was a popular actor; and the accused had been caught red-handed, as it were, by the most popular soldier of the patriotic season. In those extraordinary circumstances the Press was paralysed into probity and accuracy; and the rest of this somewhat singular business can practically be recorded from the reports of Bruno's trial.

The trial was presided over by Mr. Justice Monkhouse, one of those who are jeered at as humorous judges, but who are generally much more serious than the serious judges, for their levity comes from a living impatience of professional solemnity; while the serious judge is really filled with frivolity, because he is filled with vanity. All the chief actors being of a worldly importance, the barristers were well balanced; the prosecutor for the Crown was Sir Walter Cowdray, a heavy but weighty advocate of the sort that knows how to seem English and trustworthy, and how to be rhetorical with reluctance. The prisoner was defended by Mr. Patrick Butler, K.C., who was mistaken for a mere *flâneur* by those who misunderstand the Irish character—and those who had not been examined by him. The medical evidence involved no contradictions, the doctor whom Seymour had summoned on the spot, agreeing with the eminent surgeon who had later examined the body. Aurora Rome had been stabbed with some sharp instrument such as a knife or dagger; some instrument, at least, of which the blade was short. The wound was just over the heart, and she had died instantly. When the first doctor saw her she could hardly have been dead for twenty minutes. Therefore when Father Brown found her she could hardly have been dead for three.

Some official detective evidence followed, chiefly concerned with the presence or absence of any proof of a struggle: the only suggestion of this was the tearing of the dress at the shoulder, and this did not seem to fit in particularly well with the direction and finality of the blow. When these details had been supplied, though not explained, the first of the important witnesses was called.

Sir Wilson Seymour gave evidence as he did everything else that he did at all—not only well, but perfectly. Though himself much more of a public man than the judge, he conveyed exactly the fine shade of self-effacement before the King's Justice; and though everyone looked at him as they would at the Prime Minister or the Archbishop of Canterbury, they could have said nothing of his part in it but that it was that of a private gentleman, with an accent on the noun. He was also refreshingly lucid, as he was on the committees. He had been calling on Miss Rome at the theatre; he had met Captain Cutler there; they had been joined for a short time by the accused, who had then returned to his own dressing-room; they had then been joined by a Roman Catholic priest, who asked for the deceased lady and said his name was Brown. Miss Rome had then gone just outside the theatre to the entrance of the passage, in order to point out to Captain Cutler a flower-shop at which he was to buy her some more flowers; and the witness had remained in the room, exchanging a few words with the priest. He had then distinctly heard the deceased, having sent the Captain on his errand, turn round laughing and run down the passage towards its other end, where was the prisoner's dressing-room. In idle curiosity as to the rapid movements of his friends, he had strolled out to the head of the passage himself and looked down it towards the prisoner's door. Did he see anything in the passage? Yes, he saw something in the passage.

Sir Walter Cowdray allowed an impressive interval, during which the witness looked down, and for all his usual composure seemed to have more than his usual pallor. Then the barrister said in a lower voice, which seemed at once sympathetic and creepy: "Did you see it distinctly?"

Sir Wilson Seymour, however moved, had his excellent brains in full working order. "Very distinctly as regards its outline, but quite indistinctly—indeed not at all—as regards the details inside the outline. The passage is of such length that anyone in the middle of it appears quite black against the light at the other end." The witness lowered his steady eyes once more and added: "I had noticed the fact before, when Captain Cutler first entered it." There was another silence, and the judge leaned forward and made a note.

"Well," said Sir Walter patiently, "what was the outline like? Was it, for instance, like the figure of the murdered woman?"

"Not in the least," answered Seymour quietly.

"What did it look to you like?"

"It looked to me," replied the witness, "like a tall man."

Everyone in court kept his eyes riveted on his pen or his umbrella handle or his book or his boots or whatever he happened to be looking at. They seemed to be holding their eyes away from the prisoner by main force; but they felt his figure in the dock, and they felt it as gigantic. Tall as Bruno was to the eye, he seemed to swell taller and taller when all eyes had been torn away from him.

Cowdray was resuming his seat with his solemn face, smoothing his black silk robes and white silk whiskers. Sir Wilson was leaving the witness-box, after a few final particulars to which there were many other witnesses, when the counsel for the defence sprang up and stopped him.

"I shall only detain you a moment," said Mr. Butler, who was a rustic-looking person with red eyebrows and an expression of partial slumber. "Will you tell his lordship how you knew it was a man?"

A faint, refined smile seemed to pass over Seymour's features. "I'm afraid it is the vulgar test of trousers," he said. "When I saw daylight between the long legs I was sure it was a man, after all."

Butler's sleepy eyes opened as suddenly as some silent explosion. "After all!" he repeated slowly. "So you did think first it was a woman?"

Seymour looked troubled for the first time. "It is hardly a point of fact," he said, "but if his lordship would like me to answer for my impression, of course I shall do so. There was something about the thing that was not exactly a woman and yet was not quite a man; somehow the curves were different. And it had something that looked like long hair."

"Thank you," said Mr. Butler, K.C., and sat down suddenly, as if he had got what he wanted.

Captain Cutler was a far less plausible and composed witness than Sir Wilson, but his account of the opening incidents was solidly the same. He described the return of Bruno to his dressing-room, the dispatching of himself to buy a bunch of lilies-of-the-valley, his return to the upper end of the passage, the thing he saw in the passage, his suspicion of Seymour, and his struggle with Bruno. But he could give little artistic assistance about the black figure that he and Seymour had seen. Asked about its outline, he said he was no art critic—with a somewhat too obvious sneer at Seymour. Asked if it was a man or a woman, he said it looked more like a beast—with a too obvious snarl at the prisoner. But the man was plainly shaken with sorrow and sincere anger, and Cowdray quickly excused him from confirming facts that were already fairly clear.

The defending counsel also was again brief in his cross-examination; although (as was his custom) even in being brief, he seemed to take a long time about it. "You used a rather remarkable expression," he said, look-ing at Cutler sleepily. "What do you mean by saying that it looked more like a beast than a man or a woman?"

Cutler seemed seriously agitated. "Perhaps I oughtn't to have said that," he said, "but when the brute has huge humped shoulders like a chimpanzee, and bristles sticking out of its head like a pig——"

Mr. Butler cut short his curious impatience in the middle. "Never mind whether its hair was like a pig's," he said; "was it like a woman's?"

"A woman's!" cried the soldier. "Great Scott, no!"

"The last witness said it was," commented the counsel, with unscru-pulous swiftness. "And did the figure have any of those serpentine and semi-feminine curves to which eloquent allusion has been made? No? No feminine curves? The figure, if I understand you, was rather heavy and square than otherwise?"

"He may have been bending forward," said Cutler, in a hoarse and rather faint voice.

"Or again, he may not," said Mr. Butler, and sat down suddenly for the second time.

The third witness called by Sir Walter Cowdray was the little Catholic clergyman, so little compared with the others, that his head seemed hardly to come above the box, so that it was like cross-examining a child. But unfortunately Sir Walter had somehow got it into his head (mostly by some ramifications of his family's religion) that Father Brown was on the side of the prisoner, because the prisoner was wicked and foreign and even partly black. Therefore, he took Father Brown up sharply whenever that proud pontiff tried to explain anything; and told him to answer yes or no, and tell the plain facts without any jesuitry. When Father Brown began, in his simplicity, to say who he thought the man in the passage was, the barrister told him that he did not want his theories.

"A black shape was seen in the passage. And you say you saw the black shape. Well, what shape was it?"

Father Brown blinked as under rebuke; but he had long known the literal nature of obedience. "The shape," he said, "was short and thick, but had two sharp, black projections curved upwards on each side of the head or top, rather like horns, and——"

"Oh! the devil with horns, no doubt," ejaculated Cowdray, sitting down in triumphant jocularity. "It was the devil come to eat Protestants."

"No," said the priest dispassionately; "I know who it was."

Those in court had been wrought up to an irrational but real sense of some monstrosity. They had forgotten the figure in the dock and thought only of the figure in the passage. And the figure in the passage, described by three capable and respectable men who had all seen it, was a shifting nightmare: one called it a woman, and the other a beast, and the other a devil. . . .

The judge was looking at Father Brown with level and piercing eyes. "You are a most extraordinary witness," he said, "but there is something about you that makes me think you are trying to tell the truth. Well, who was the man you saw in the passage?"

"He was myself," said Father Brown.

Butler, K.C., sprang to his feet in an extraordinary stillness, and said quite calmly: "Your lordship will allow me to cross-examine?" And then, without stopping, he shot at Brown the apparently disconnected question: "You have heard about this dagger; you know the experts say the crime was committed with a short blade?"

"A short blade," assented Brown, nodding solemnly like an owl, "but a very long hilt."

Before the audience could quite dismiss the idea that the priest had really seen himself doing murder with a short dagger with a long hilt (which seemed somehow to make it more horrible), he had himself hurried on to explain.

"I mean daggers aren't the only things with short blades. Spears have short blades. And spears catch at the end of the steel just like daggers, if they're that sort of fancy spear they have in theatres; like the spear poor old Parkinson killed his wife with, just when she'd sent for me to settle their family troubles—and I came just too late, God forgive me! But he died penitent—he just died of being penitent. He couldn't bear what he'd done."

The general impression in court was that the little priest, who was gabbling away, had literally gone mad in the box. But the judge still looked at him with bright and steady eyes of interest; and the counsel for the defence went on with his questions, unperturbed.

"If Parkinson did it with that pantomime spear," asked Butler, "he must have thrust from four yards away. How do you account for signs of struggle, like the dress dragged off the shoulder?" He had slipped into treating this mere witness as an expert; but no one noticed it now.

"The poor lady's dress was torn," said the witness, "because it was caught in a panel that slid to just behind her. She struggled to free herself, and as she did so Parkinson came out of the prisoner's room and lunged with the spear."

"A panel?" repeated the barrister in a curious voice.

"It was a looking-glass on the other side," explained Father Brown. "When I was in the dressing-room I noticed that some of them could probably be slid out into the passage."

There was another vast and unnatural silence, and this time it was the judge who spoke. "So you really mean that, when you looked down that passage, the man you saw was yourself—in a mirror?"

"Yes, my lord; that was what I was trying to say," said Brown, "but they asked me for the shape; and our hats have corners just like horns, and so I——"

The judge leaned forward, his old eyes yet more brilliant, and said in specially distinct tones: "Do you really mean to say that when Sir Wilson Seymour saw that wild what-you-call-him with curves and a woman's hair and a man's trousers, what he saw was Sir Wilson Seymour?"

"Yes, my lord," said Father Brown.

"And you mean to say that when Captain Cutler saw that chimpanzee with humped shoulders and hog's bristles, he simply saw himself?"

"Yes, my lord."

The judge leaned back in his chair with a luxuriance in which it was hard to separate the cynicism and the admiration. "And can you tell us why," he asked, "you should know your own figure in a looking-glass, when two such distinguished men don't?"

Father Brown blinked even more painfully than before; then he stammered: "Really, my lord, I don't know . . . unless it's because I don't look at it so often."

The Perishing of the Pendragons

FATHER BROWN WAS in no mood for adventures. He had lately fallen ill with over-work, and when he began to recover, his friend Flambeau had taken him on a cruise in a small yacht with Sir Cecil Fanshaw, a young Cornish squire and an enthusiast for Cornish coast scenery. But Brown was still rather weak; he was no very happy sailor; and though he was never of the sort that either grumbles or breaks down, his spirits did not rise above patience and civility. When the other two men praised the ragged violet sunset or the ragged volcanic crags, he agreed with them. When Flambeau pointed out a rock shaped like a dragon, he looked at it and thought it very like a dragon. When Fanshaw more excitedly indicated a rock that was like Merlin he looked at it, and signified assent. When Flambeau asked whether this rocky gate of the twisted river was not the gate of Fairyland, he said "Yes." He heard the most important things and the most trivial with the same tasteless absorption. He heard that the coast was death to all but careful seamen; he also heard that the ship's cat was asleep. He heard that Fanshaw couldn't find his cigar-holder anywhere; he also heard the pilot deliver the oracle "Both eyes bright, she's all right; one eye winks, down she sinks." He heard Flambeau say to Fanshaw that no doubt this meant the pilot must keep both eyes open and be spry. And he heard Fanshaw say to Flambeau that, oddly enough, it didn't mean this: it meant that while they saw two of the coast-lights, one near and the other distant, exactly side by side, they were in the right river-channel; but that if one light was hidden behind the other, they were going on the rocks. He heard Fanshaw add that his county was full of such quaint fables and idioms; it was the very home of romance; he even pitted this part of Cornwall against Devonshire, as a claimant to the laurels of Elizabethan seamanship. According to him there had been captains among these coves and islets compared with whom Drake was practically a landsman. He heard Flambeau laugh, and ask if, perhaps, the adventurous title of "Westward Ho!" only meant that all Devonshire men wished they were living in Cornwall. He heard Fanshaw say there was no need to be silly; that not only had Cornish captains been heroes, but that they were heroes still: that near that very spot there was an old admiral, now retired, who was scarred by thrilling voyages full of adventures; and who had in his youth found the last group of eight Pacific Islands that was added to the chart of the world. This Cecil Fanshaw was, in person, of the kind that commonly urges such crude but pleasing enthusiasms; a very young man, light-haired, high-coloured, with an eager profile; with a boyish bravado of spirits, but an almost girlish delicacy of tint and type. The big shoulders, black brows and black mousquetaire swagger of Flambeau were a great contrast.

All these trivialities Brown heard and saw; but heard them as a tired man hears a tune in the railway wheels or saw them as a sick man sees the pattern of his wall-paper. No one can calculate the turns of mood in convalescence; but Father Brown's depression must have had a great deal to do with his mere unfamiliarity with the sea. For as the river-mouth narrowed like the neck of a bottle, and the water grew calmer and the air warmer and more earthy, he seemed to wake up and take notice like a baby. They had reached that phase just after sunset when air and water both look bright, but earth and all its growing things look almost black by comparison. About this particular evening, however, there was something exceptional. It was one of those rare atmospheres in which a smoked glass slide seems to have been slid away from between us and Nature; so that even dark colours on that day look more gorgeous than bright colours on cloudier days. The trampled earth of the river-banks and the peaty stain in the pools did not look drab but glowing umber, and the dark woods astir in the breeze did not look, as usual, dim blue with mere depth or distance, but more like wind-tumbled masses of some vivid violet blossom. This magic clearness and intensity in the colours was further forced on Brown's slowly reviving senses by something romantic and even secret in the very form of the landscape.

The river was still well wide and deep enough for a pleasure boat so small as theirs; but the curves of the country-side suggested that it was closing in on either hand; the woods seemed to be making broken and flying attempts at bridge-building; as if the boat were passing from the romance of a valley to the romance of a hollow and so to the supreme romance of a tunnel. Beyond this mere look of things there was little for Brown's freshening fancy to feed on; he saw no human beings, except some gypsies trailing along the river-bank, with faggots and osiers cut in the forest; and one sight no longer unconventional, but in such remote parts still uncommon: a dark-haired lady bare-headed, and paddling her own canoe. If Father Brown ever attached any importance to either of these, he certainly forgot them at the next turn of the river, which brought in sight a singular object.

The water seemed to widen and split, being cloven by the dark wedge of a fish-shaped and wooded islet. With the rate at which they went, the islet seemed to swim towards them like a ship; a ship with a very high prow—or, to speak more strictly, a very high funnel. For at the extreme point nearest them stood up an odd-looking building, unlike anything they could remember or connect with any purpose. It was not specially high, but it was too high for its breadth to be called anything but a tower. Yet it appeared to be built entirely of wood, and that in a most unequal and eccentric way. Some of the planks and beams were of good, seasoned oak; some of such wood cut raw and recent; some again of white pine-wood and a great deal more of the same sort of wood painted black with tar. These black beams were set crooked or criss-cross at all kinds of angles; giving the whole a most patchy and puzzling appearance. There were one or two windows, which appeared to be coloured and leaded in an old-fashioned but more elaborate style. The travellers looked at it with that paradoxical feeling we have when something reminds us of something, and yet we are certain it is something very different.

Father Brown, even when he was mystified, was clever in analysing his own mystification. And he found himself reflecting that the oddity seemed to consist in a particular shape cut out in an incongruous material; as if one saw a top-hat made of tin or a frock-coat cut out of tartan. He was sure he had seen timbers of different tints arranged like that somewhere, but never in such architectural proportions. The next moment a glimpse through the dark trees told him all he wanted to know; and he laughed. Through a gap in the foliage there appeared for a moment one of those old wooden houses, faced with black beams, which are still to be found here and there in England, but which most of us see imitated in some show called "Old London" or "Shakespeare's England." It was in view only long enough for the priest to see that, however old-fashioned, it was a comfortable and well-kept country-house, with flower beds in front of it. It had none of the piebald and crazy look of the tower that seemed made out of its refuse.

"What on earth's this?" said Flambeau, who was still staring at the tower.

Fanshaw's eyes were shining and he spoke triumphantly. "Aha, you've not seen a place quite like this before, I fancy; that's why I've brought you here, my friend. Now you shall see whether I exaggerate about the mariners of Cornwall. This place belongs to Old Pendragon, whom we call the Admiral; though he retired before getting the rank. The spirit of

Raleigh and Hawkins is a memory with the Devon folk; it's a modern fact
with the Pendragons. If Queen Elizabeth were to rise from the grave and
come up this river in a gilded barge, she would be received by the
Admiral in a house exactly such as she was accustomed to, in every
corner and casement, in every panel on the wall or plate on the table.
And she would find an English Captain still talking fiercely of fresh lands
to be found in little ships, as much as if she had dined with Drake."

"She'd find a rum sort of thing in the garden," said Father Brown,
"which would not please her Renaissance eye. That Elizabethan domestic architecture is charming in its way; but it's against the very nature of it
to break out into turrets."

"And yet," answered Fanshaw, "that's the most romantic and Elizabethan part of the business. It was built by the Pendragons in the very
days of the Spanish wars; and though it's needed patching and even
rebuilding for another reason, it's always been rebuilt in the old way. The
story goes that the lady of Sir Peter Pendragon built it in this place and to
this height, because from the top you can just see the corner where vessels
turn into the river-mouth; and she wished to be the first to see her
husband's ship, as he sailed home from the Spanish main."

"For what other reason," asked Father Brown, "do you mean that it has
been rebuilt?"

"Oh, there's a strange story about that too," said the young squire with
relish. "You are really in a land of strange stories; King Arthur was here
and Merlin and the fairies before him. The story goes that Sir Peter
Pendragon, who (I fear) had some of the faults of the pirates as well as the
virtues of the sailor, was bringing home three Spanish gentlemen in
honourable captivity, intending to escort them to Elizabeth's court. But
he was a man of flaming and tigerish temper; and coming to high words
with one of them, he caught him by the throat and flung him, by
accident or design, into the sea. A second Spaniard, who was the brother
of the first, instantly drew his sword and flew at Pendragon, and after a
short but furious combat in which both got three wounds in as many
minutes, Pendragon drove his blade through the other's body and the
second Spaniard was accounted for. As it happened the ship had already
turned into the river-mouth and was close to comparatively shallow
water. The third Spaniard sprang over the side of the ship, struck out for
the shore, and was soon near enough to it to stand up to his waist in water.
And turning again to face the ship, and holding up both arms to Heaven
like a prophet calling plagues upon a wicked city, he called out to
Pendragon in a piercing and terrible voice, that he at least was yet living,
that he would go on living, that he would live for ever; and that generation after generation the house of Pendragon should never see him or his,

but should know by very certain signs that he and his vengeance were alive. With that he dived under the wave, and was either drowned or swam so long under water that no hair of his head was seen afterwards."

"There's that girl in the canoe again," said Flambeau irrelevantly, for good-looking young women would call him off any topic. "She seems bothered by the queer tower just as we were."

Indeed, the black-haired young lady was letting her canoe float slowly and silently past the strange islet; and was looking intently up at the strange tower, with a strong glow of curiosity on her oval and olive face.

"Never mind girls," said Fanshaw impatiently, "there are plenty of them in the world, but not many things like the Pendragon Tower. As you may easily suppose, plenty of superstitions and scandals have followed in the track of the Spaniard's curse; and no doubt, as you would put it, any accident happening to this Cornish family would be connected with it by rural credulity. But it is perfectly true that this tower has been burnt down two or three times; and the family can't be called lucky, for more than two, I think, of the Admiral's near kin have perished by shipwreck; and one at least, to my own knowledge, on practically the same spot where Sir Peter threw the Spaniard overboard."

"What a pity!" exclaimed Flambeau. "She's going."

"When did your friend the Admiral tell you this family history?" asked Father Brown, as the girl in the canoe paddled off, without showing the least intention of extending her interest from the tower to the yacht, which Fanshaw had already caused to lie alongside the island.

"Many years ago," replied Fanshaw; "he hasn't been to sea for some time now, though he is as keen on it as ever. I believe there's a family compact or something. Well, here's the landing-stage; let's come ashore and see the old boy."

They followed him on to the island just under the tower; and Father Brown, whether from the mere touch of dry land, or the interest of something on the other bank of the river (which he stared at very hard for some seconds), seemed singularly improved in briskness. They entered a wooded avenue between two fences of thin greyish wood, such as often enclose parks or gardens; and over the top of which the dark trees tossed to and fro like black and purple plumes upon the hearse of a giant. The tower, as they left it behind, looked all the quainter, because such entrances are usually flanked by two towers; and this one looked lop-sided. But for this, the avenue had the usual appearance of the entrance to a gentleman's grounds; and, being so curved that the house was now out of sight, somehow looked a much larger park than any plantation on such an island could really be. Father Brown was, perhaps, a little fanciful in his fatigue, but he almost thought the whole place must be growing larger, as things do in a nightmare. Anyhow, a mystical monotony was the only character of their march, until Fanshaw suddenly stopped, and pointed to something sticking out through the grey fence—something that looked at first rather like the imprisoned horn of some beast. Closer observation showed that it was a slightly curved blade of metal that shone faintly in the fading light.

Flambeau, who like all Frenchmen had been a soldier, bent over it and said in a startled voice: "Why, it's a sabre! I believe I know the sort; heavy and curved, but shorter than the cavalry; they used to have them in the artillery and the——"

As he spoke the blade plucked itself out of the crack it had made and came down again with a more ponderous slash, splitting the fissiparous fence to the bottom, with a rending noise. Then it was pulled out again, flashed above the fence some feet farther along, and again split it half-way down with the first stroke; and after waggling a little to extricate itself (accompanied with curses in the darkness) split it down to the ground with a second. Then a kick of devilish energy sent the whole loosened square of thin wood flying into the pathway, and a great gap of dark coppice gaped in the paling.

Fanshaw peered into the dark opening, and uttered an exclamation of astonishment. "My dear Admiral!" he exclaimed, "do you—er—do you generally cut out a new front door whenever you want to go for a walk?"

The voice in the gloom swore again, and then broke into a jolly laugh. "No," it said; "I've really got to cut down this fence somehow; it's spoiling all the plants, and no one else here can do it. But I'll only carve another bit off the front door, and then come out and welcome you."

And sure enough, he heaved up his weapon once more, and, hacking twice, brought down another and similar strip of fence, making the opening about fourteen feet wide in all. Then through this larger forest gateway he came out into the evening light, with a chip of grey wood sticking to his sword-blade.

He momentarily fulfilled all Fanshaw's fable of an old piratical Admiral; though the details seemed afterwards to decompose into accidents. For instance, he wore an ordinary broad-brimmed hat as against the sun; but the front flap of it was turned up straight to the sky and the two corners pulled down lower than the ears; so that it stood across his forehead in a crescent like the old cocked hat worn by Nelson. He wore an ordinary dark-blue jacket, with nothing special about the buttons, but the combination of it with white linen trousers somehow had a sailorish look. He was tall and loose, and walked with a sort of swagger, which was not a sailor's roll, and yet somehow suggested it. And he held in his hand a short sabre which was like a navy cutlass, but about twice as big. Under

the bridge of the hat, his eagle face looked eager, all the more because it
was not only clean-shaven, but without eyebrows. It seemed almost as if
all the hair had come off his face from his thrusting it through a throng of
elements. His eyes were prominent and piercing. His colour was curiously attractive, while partly tropical; it reminded one vaguely of a blood-
orange. That is, that while it was ruddy and sanguine, there was a yellow
in it that was in no way sickly, but seemed rather to glow like gold apples
of the Hesperides. Father Brown thought he had never seen a figure so
expressive of all the romances about the countries of the Sun.

When Fanshaw had presented his two friends to their host, he fell
again into a tone of rallying the latter about his wreckage of the fence and
his apparent rage of profanity. The Admiral pooh-poohed it at first as a
piece of necessary but annoying garden work; but at length the ring of
real energy came back into his laughter, and he cried with a mixture of
impatience and good humour:

"Well, perhaps I do go at it a bit rabidly, and feel a kind of pleasure in
smashing anything. So would you if your only pleasure was in cruising
about to find some new Cannibal Islands, and you had to stick on this
muddy little rockery in a sort of rustic pond. When I remember how I've
cut down a mile and a half of green poisonous jungle with an old cutlass
half as sharp as this; and then remember I must stop here and chop this
matchwood, because of some confounded old bargain scribbled in a
family Bible, why, I——"

He swung up the heavy steel again; and this time sundered the wall of
wood from top to bottom at one stroke.

"I feel like that," he said laughing, but furiously flinging the sword
some yards down the path, "and now let's go up to the house; you must
have some dinner."

The semicircle of lawn in front of the house was varied by three
circular garden beds, one of red tulips, a second of yellow tulips, and the
third of some white waxen-looking blossoms that the visitors did not
know and presumed to be exotic. A heavy, hairy and rather sullen-
looking gardener was hanging up a heavy coil of garden hose. The
corners of the expiring sunset which seemed to cling about the corners of
the house gave glimpses here and there of the colours of remoter flower
beds; and in a treeless space on one side of the house opening upon the
river stood a tall brass tripod on which was tilted a big brass telescope. Just
outside the steps of the porch stood a little painted green garden table, as
if someone had just had tea there. The entrance was flanked with two of
those half-featured lumps of stone with holes for eyes that are said to be
South Sea idols; and on the brown oak beam across the doorway were
some confused carvings that looked almost as barbaric.

As they passed indoors, the little cleric hopped suddenly on to the table, and standing on it peered unaffectedly through the spectacles at the mouldings in the oak. Admiral Pendragon looked very much astonished, though not particularly annoyed; while Fanshaw was so amused with what looked like a performing pigmy on his little stand, that he could not control his laughter. But Father Brown was not likely to notice either the laughter or the astonishment.

He was gazing at three carved symbols, which, though very worn and obscure, seemed still to convey some sense to him. The first seemed to be the outline of some tower or other building, crowned with what looked like curly pointed ribbons. The second was clearer; an old Elizabethan galley with decorative waves beneath it, but interrupted in the middle by a curious jagged rock, which was either a fault in the wood or some conventional representation of the water coming in. The third represented the upper half of a human figure, ending in an escalloped line like the waves; the face was rubbed and featureless; and both arms were held very stiffly up in the air.

"Well," muttered Father Brown, blinking, "here is the legend of the Spaniard plain enough. Here he is holding up his arms and cursing in the sea; and here are the two curses: the wrecked ship and the burning of Pendragon Tower."

Pendragon shook his head with a kind of venerable amusement. "And how many other things might it not be?" he said. "Don't you know that that sort of half man, like a half lion or half stag, is quite common in heraldry? Might not that line through the ship be one of those *parti-per-pale* lines, *indented*, I think they call it? And though the third thing isn't very heraldic, it would be more heraldic to suppose it a tower crowned with laurel than with fire; and it looks just as like it."

"But it seems rather odd," said Flambeau, "that it should exactly confirm the old legend."

"Ah," replied the sceptical traveller, "but you don't know how much of the old legend may have been made up from the old figures. Besides, it isn't the only old legend. Fanshaw, here, who is fond of such things, will tell you there are other versions of the tale, and much more horrible ones. One story credits my unfortunate ancestor with having had the Spaniard cut in two; and that will fit the pretty picture also. Another obligingly credits our family with the possession of a tower full of snakes and explains those little, wriggly things in that way. And a third theory supposes the crooked line on the ship to be a conventionalised thunderbolt; but that alone, if seriously examined, would show what a very little way these unhappy coincidences really go."

"Why, how do you mean?" asked Fanshaw.

"It so happens," replied his host coolly, "that there was no thunder and lightning at all in the two or three shipwrecks I know of in our family."

"Oh!" said Father Brown, and jumped down from the little table.

There was another silence in which they heard the continuous murmur of the river; then Fanshaw said, in a doubtful and perhaps disappointed tone: "Then you don't think there is anything in the tales of the tower in flames?"

"There are the tales, of course," said the Admiral, shrugging his shoulders, "and some of them, I don't deny, on evidence as decent as one ever gets for such things. Someone saw a blaze hereabout, don't you know, as he walked home through a wood; someone keeping sheep on the uplands inland thought he saw a flame hovering over Pendragon tower. Well, a damp dab of mud like this confounded island seems the last place where one would think of fires."

"What is that fire over there?" asked Father Brown, with a gentle suddenness pointing to the woods on the left river-bank. They were all thrown a little off their balance, and the more fanciful Fanshaw had even some difficulty in recovering his, as they saw a long, thin stream of blue smoke ascending silently into the end of the evening light.

Then Pendragon broke into a scornful laugh again. "Gypsies!" he said; "they've been camping about here for a week. Gentlemen, you want your dinner," and he turned as if to enter the house.

But the antiquarian superstition in Fanshaw was still quivering; and he said hastily, "But, Admiral, what's that hissing noise quite near the island? It's very like fire."

"It's more like what it is," said the Admiral, laughing as he led the way; "it's only some canoe going by."

Almost as he spoke the butler, a lean man in black, with very black hair and a very long, yellow face, appeared in the doorway and told him that dinner was served.

The dining-room was as nautical as the cabin of a ship; but its note was rather that of the modern than the Elizabethan captain. There were, indeed, three antiquated cutlasses in a trophy over the fireplace and one brown sixteenth-century map, with Tritons and little ships dotted about a curly sea. But such things were less prominent on the white panelling than some cases of quaint coloured South American birds, very scientifically stuffed, fantastic shells from the Pacific, and several instruments so rude and queer in shape that savages might have used them either to kill their enemies or to cook them. But the alien colour culminated in the fact that, besides the butler, the Admiral's only servants were two negroes, somewhat quaintly clad in tight uniforms of yellow. The priest's instinctive trick of analysing his own impressions told him that the colour and the little neat coat-tails of these bipeds had suggested the word "Canary," and so by a mere pun connected them with Southward travel. Towards the end of the dinner they took their yellow clothes and black faces out of the room, leaving only the black clothes and yellow face of the butler.

"I'm rather sorry you take this so lightly," said Fanshaw to the host, "for the truth is I've brought these friends of mine with the idea of their helping you, as they know a good deal of these things. Don't you really believe in the family story at all?"

"I don't believe in anything," answered Pendragon very briskly, with a bright eye cocked at a red tropical bird. "I'm a man of science."

Rather to Flambeau's surprise, his clerical friend, who seemed to have entirely woke up, took up the digression and talked natural history with his host with a flow of words and much unexpected information, until the dessert and decanters were set down and the last of the servants vanished. Then he said, without altering his tone:

"Please don't think me impertinent, Admiral Pendragon. I don't ask for curiosity, but really for my guidance and your convenience. Have I made a bad shot if I guess you don't want these old things talked of before your butler?"

The Admiral lifted the hairless arches over his eyes and exclaimed, "Well, I don't know where you got it; but the truth is I can't stand the fellow, though I've no excuse for discharging a family servant. Fanshaw, with his fairy tales, would say my blood moved against men with that black, Spanish-looking hair."

Flambeau struck the table with his heavy fist. "By Jove!" he cried, "and so had that girl!"

"I hope it'll all end to-night," continued the Admiral, "when my nephew comes back safe from his ship. You look surprised. You won't understand, I suppose, unless I tell you the story. You see, my father had two sons; I remained a bachelor, but my elder brother married, and had a son who became a sailor like all the rest of us, and will inherit the proper estate. Well, my father was a strange man; he somehow combined Fanshaw's superstition with a good deal of my scepticism; they were always fighting in him; and after my first voyages, he developed a notion which he thought somehow would settle finally whether the curse was truth or trash. If all the Pendragons sailed about anyhow, he thought there would be too much chance of natural catastrophes to prove anything. But if we went to sea one at a time in strict order of succession to the property, he thought it might show whether any connected fate followed the family as a family. It was a silly notion, I think, and I quarrelled with my father pretty heartily; for I was an ambitious man and was left to the last, coming, by succession, after my own nephew."

"And your father and brother," said the priest, very gently, "died at sea, I fear."

"Yes," groaned the Admiral; "by one of those brutal accidents on which are built all the lying mythologies of mankind, they were both shipwrecked. My father, coming up this coast out of the Atlantic, was washed up on these Cornish rocks. My brother's ship was sunk, no one knows where, on the voyage home from Tasmania. His body was never found. I tell you it was from perfectly natural mishap; lots of other people besides Pendragons were drowned; and both disasters are discussed in a normal way by navigators. But, of course, it set this forest of superstition on fire; and men saw the flaming tower everywhere. That's why I say it will be all right when Walter returns. The girl he's engaged to was coming to-day; but I was so afraid of some chance delay frightening her that I wired her not to come till she heard from me. But he's practically sure to be here some time to-night; and then it'll all end in smoke—tobacco smoke. We'll crack that old lie when we crack a bottle of this wine."

"Very good wine," said Father Brown, gravely lifting his glass, "but, as you see, a very bad wine-bibber. I most sincerely beg your pardon": for he had spilt a small spot of wine on the table-cloth. He drank and put down the glass with a composed face; but his hand had started at the exact moment when he became conscious of a face looking in through the garden window just behind the Admiral—the face of a woman, swarthy, with Southern hair and eyes, and young, but like a mask of tragedy.

After a pause the priest spoke again in his mild manner. "Admiral," he said, "will you do me a favour? Let me, and my friends if they like, stop in that tower of yours just for to-night? Do you know that in my business you're an exorcist almost before anything else?"

Pendragon sprang to his feet and paced swiftly to and fro across the window, from which the face had instantly vanished. "I tell you there is nothing in it," he cried, with ringing violence. "There is one thing I know about this matter. You may call me an atheist. I am an atheist." Here he swung round and fixed Father Brown with a face of frightful concentration. "This business is perfectly natural. There is no curse in it at all."

Father Brown smiled. "In that case," he said, "there can't be any objection to my sleeping in your delightful summer-house."

"The idea is utterly ridiculous," replied the Admiral, beating a tattoo on the back of his chair.

"Please forgive me for everything," said Brown in his most sympathetic tone, "including spilling the wine. But it seems to me you are not quite so easy about the flaming tower as you try to be."

Admiral Pendragon sat down again as abruptly as he had risen; but he sat quite still, and when he spoke again it was in a lower voice. "You do it at your own peril," he said; "but wouldn't *you* be an atheist to keep sane in all this devilry?"

Some three hours afterwards Fanshaw, Flambeau and the priest were still dawdling about the garden in the dark; and it began to dawn on the other two that Father Brown had no intention of going to bed either in the tower or the house.

"I think the lawn wants weeding," said he dreamily. "If I could find a spud or something I'd do it myself."

They followed him, laughing and half remonstrating; but he replied with the utmost solemnity, explaining to them, in a maddening little sermon, that one can always find some small occupation that is helpful to others. He did not find a spud; but he found an old broom made of twigs, with which he began most energetically to brush the fallen leaves off the grass.

"Always some little thing to be done," he said with idiot cheerfulness; "as George Herbert says, 'Who sweeps an Admiral's garden in Cornwall as for Thy laws makes that and the action fine.' And now," he added, suddenly slinging the broom away, "let's go and water the flowers."

With the same mixed emotions, they watched him uncoil some considerable lengths of the large garden hose, saying with an air of wistful discrimination, "The red tulips before the yellow, I think. Look a bit dry, don't you think?"

He turned the little tap on the instrument, and the water shot out straight and solid as a long rod of steel.

"Look out, Samson," cried Flambeau; "why, you've cut off the tulip's head."

Father Brown stood ruefully contemplating the decapitated plant.

"Mine does seem to be a rather kill or cure sort of watering," he admitted, scratching his head. "I suppose it's a pity I didn't find the spud. You should have seen me with the spud! Talking of tools, you've got that swordstick, Flambeau, you always carry? That's right; and Sir Cecil could have that sword the Admiral threw away by the fence here. How grey everything looks!"

"The mist's rising from the river," said the staring Flambeau.

Almost as he spoke the huge figure of the hairy gardener appeared on a higher ridge of the trenched and terraced lawn, hailing them with a brandished rake and a horribly bellowing voice. "Put down that hose," he shouted; "put down that hose and go to your——"

"I am fearfully clumsy," replied the reverend gentleman weakly; "do you know, I upset some wine at dinner." He made a wavering half-turn of apology towards the gardener, with the hose still spouting in his hand. The gardener caught the cold crash of the water full in his face like the crash of a cannon-ball; staggered, slipped and went sprawling with his boots in the air.

"How very dreadful!" said Father Brown, looking round in a sort of wonder. "Why, I've hit a man!"

He stood with his head forward for a moment as if looking or listening; and then set off at a trot towards the tower, still trailing the hose behind him. The tower was quite close, but its outline was curiously dim.

"Your river mist," he said, "has a rum smell."

"By the Lord it has," cried Fanshaw, who was very white. "But you can't mean——"

"I mean," said Father Brown, "that one of the Admiral's scientific predictions is coming true to-night. This story is going to end in smoke."

As he spoke a most beautiful rose-red light seemed to burst into blossom like a gigantic rose; but accompanied with a crackling and rattling noise that was like the laughter of devils.

"My God! what is this?" cried Sir Cecil Fanshaw.

"The sign of the flaming tower," said Father Brown, and sent the driving water from his hose into the heart of the red patch.

"Lucky we hadn't gone to bed!" ejaculated Fanshaw. "I suppose it can't spread to the house."

"You may remember," said the priest quietly, "that the wooden fence that might have carried it was cut away."

Flambeau turned electrified eyes upon his friend, but Fanshaw only said rather absently, "Well, nobody can be killed, anyhow."

"This is rather a curious kind of tower," observed Father Brown; "when it takes to killing people, it always kills people who are somewhere else."

At the same instant the monstrous figure of the gardener with the streaming beard stood again on the green ridge against the sky, waving others to come on; but now waving not a rake but a cutlass. Behind him came the two negroes, also with the old crooked cutlasses out of the trophy. But in the blood-red glare, with their black faces and yellow figures, they looked like devils carrying instruments of torture. In the dim garden behind them a distant voice was heard calling out brief directions. When the priest heard the voice, a terrible change came over his countenance.

But he remained composed; and never took his eye off the patch of flame which had begun by spreading, but now seemed to shrink a little as it hissed under the torch of the long silver spear of water. He kept his finger along the nozzle of the pipe to ensure the aim, and attended to no other business, knowing only by the noise and that semi-conscious corner of the eye, the exciting incidents that began to tumble themselves about the island garden. He gave two brief directions to his friends. One was,

"Knock these fellows down somehow and tie them up, whoever they are; there's rope down by those faggots. They want to take away my nice hose." The other was, "As soon as you get a chance, call out to that canoeing girl; she's over on the bank with the gypsies. Ask her if they could get some buckets across and fill them from the river." Then he closed his mouth and continued to water the new red flower as ruthlessly as he had watered the red tulip.

He never turned his head to look at the strange fight that followed between the foes and friends of the mysterious fire. He almost felt the island shake when Flambeau collided with the huge gardener; he merely imagined how it would whirl round them as they wrestled. He heard the crashing fall; and his friend's gasp of triumph as he dashed on to the first negro; and the cries of both the blacks as Flambeau and Fanshaw bound them. Flambeau's enormous strength more than re-dressed the odds in the fight, especially as the fourth man still hovered near the house, only a shadow and a voice. He heard also the water broken by the paddles of a canoe; the girl's voice giving orders, the voices of gypsies answering and coming nearer, the plumping and sucking noise of empty buckets plunged into a full stream; and finally the sound of many feet around the fire. But all this was less to him than the fact that the red rent, which had lately once more increased, had once more slightly diminished.

Then came a cry that very nearly made him turn his head. Flambeau and Fanshaw, now reinforced by some of the gypsies, had rushed after the mysterious man by the house; and he heard from the other end of the garden the Frenchman's cry of horror and astonishment. It was echoed by a howl not to be called human, as the being broke from their hold and ran along the garden. Three times at least it raced round the whole island, in a way that was as horrible as the chase of a lunatic, both in the cries of the pursued and the ropes carried by the pursuers; but was more horrible still, because it somehow suggested one of the chasing games of children in a garden. Then, finding them closing in on every side, the figure sprang upon one of the higher river banks and disappeared with a splash into the dark and driving river.

"You can do no more, I fear," said Brown in a voice cold with pain. "He has been washed down to the rocks by now, where he has sent so many others. He knew the use of a family legend."

"Oh, don't talk in these parables," cried Flambeau impatiently. "Can't you put it simply in words of one syllable?"

"Yes," answered Brown, with his eye on the hose. " 'Both eyes bright, she's all right; one eye blinks, down she sinks.' "

The fire hissed and shrieked more and more, like a strangled thing, as it grew narrower and narrower under the flood from the pipe and buckets, but Father Brown still kept his eye on it as he went on speaking:

"I thought of asking this young lady if it were morning yet, to look through that telescope at the river-mouth and the river. She might have seen something to interest her: the sign of the ship; or Mr. Walter Pendragon coming home; and perhaps even the sign of the half-man, for though he is certainly safe by now, he may very well have waded ashore. He has been within a shave of another shipwreck; and would never have escaped it, if the lady hadn't had the sense to suspect the old Admiral's telegram and come down to watch him. Don't let's talk about the old Admiral. Don't let's talk about anything. It's enough to say that whenever this tower, with its pitch and resin-wood, really caught fire, the spark on the horizon always looked like the twin light to the coast lighthouse."

"And that," said Flambeau, "is how the father and brother died. The wicked uncle of the legends very nearly got his estate, after all."

Father Brown did not answer; indeed, he did not speak again, save for civilities, till they were all safe round a cigar-box in the cabin of the yacht. He saw that the frustrate fire was extinguished; and then refused to linger, though he actually heard young Pendragon, escorted by an enthusiastic crowd, come tramping up the river-bank; and might (had he been moved by romantic curiosities) have received the combined thanks of the man from the ship and the girl from the canoe. But his fatigue had fallen on him once more; and he only started once, when Flambeau abruptly told him he had dropped cigar-ash on his trousers.

"That's no cigar-ash," he said rather wearily. "That's from the fire, but you don't think so because you're all smoking cigars. That's just the way I got my first faint suspicion about the chart."

"Do you mean Pendragon's chart of his Pacific Islands?" asked Fanshaw.

"You thought it was a chart of the Pacific Islands," answered Brown. "Put a feather with a fossil and a bit of coral and everyone will think it's a specimen. Put the same feather with a ribbon and an artificial flower and everyone will think it's for a lady's hat. Put the same feather with an ink-bottle, a book, and a stack of writing-paper, and most men will swear they've seen a quill pen. So you saw that map among tropic birds and shells and thought it was a map of Pacific Islands. It was the map of this river."

"But how do you know?" asked Fanshaw.

"I saw the rock you thought was like a dragon, and the one like Merlin, and——"

"You seem to have noticed a lot as we came in," cried Fanshaw. "We thought you were rather abstracted."

"I was sea-sick," said Father Brown simply. "I felt simply horrible. But feeling horrible has nothing to do with not seeing things." And he closed his eyes.

"Do you think most men would have seen that?" asked Flambeau. He received no answer: Father Brown was asleep.

The Salad of Colonel Cray

FATHER BROWN WAS walking home from Mass on a white weird morning when the mists were slowly lifting—one of those mornings when the very element of light appears as something mysterious and new. The scattered trees outlined themselves more and more out of the vapour, as if they were first drawn in grey chalk and then in charcoal. At yet more distant intervals appeared the houses upon the broken fringe of the suburb; their outlines became clearer and clearer until he recognised many in which he had chance acquaintances, and many more the names of whose owners he knew. But all the windows and doors were sealed; none of the people were of the sort that would be up at such a time, or still less on such an errand. But as he passed under the shadow of one handsome villa with verandas and wide ornate gardens, he heard a noise that made him almost involuntarily stop. It was the unmistakable noise of a pistol or carbine or some light firearm discharged; but it was not this that puzzled him most. The first full noise was immediately followed by a series of fainter noises—as he counted them, about six. He supposed it must be the echo; but the odd thing was that the echo was not in the least like the original sound. It was not like anything else that he could think of; the three things nearest to it seemed to be the noise made by siphons of soda-water, one of the many noises made by an animal, and the noise made by a person attempting to conceal laughter. None of which seemed to make much sense.

Father Brown was made of two men. There was a man of action, who was as modest as a primrose and as punctual as a clock; who went his small round of duties and never dreamed of altering it. There was also a man of reflection, who was much simpler but much stronger, who could not easily be stopped; whose thought was always (in the only intelligent sense of the words) free thought. He could not help, even unconsciously, asking himself all the questions that there were to be asked, and answer-

78

ing as many of them as he could; all that went on like his breathing or circulation. But he never consciously carried his actions outside the sphere of his own duty; and in this case the two attitudes were aptly tested. He was just about to resume his trudge in the twilight, telling himself it was no affair of his, but instinctively twisting and untwisting twenty theories about what the odd noises might mean. Then the grey sky-line brightened into silver, and in the broadening light he realised that he had been to the house which belonged to an Anglo-Indian Major named Putnam; and that the Major had a native cook from Malta who was of his communion. He also began to remember that pistol-shots are sometimes serious things; accompanied with consequences with which he was legitimately concerned. He turned back and went in at the garden gate, making for the front door.

Half-way down one side of the house stood out a projection like a very low shed; it was, as he afterwards discovered, a large dustbin. Round the corner of this came a figure, at first a mere shadow in the haze, apparently bending and peering about. Then, coming nearer, it solidified into a figure that was, indeed, rather unusually solid. Major Putnam was a bald-headed, bull-necked man, short and very broad, with one of those rather apoplectic faces that are produced by a prolonged attempt to combine the oriental climate with the occidental luxuries. But the face was a good-humoured one, and even now, though evidently puzzled and inquisitive, wore a kind of innocent grin. He had a large palm-leaf hat on the back of his head (suggesting a halo that was by no means appropriate to the face), but otherwise he was clad only in a very vivid suit of striped scarlet and yellow pyjamas; which, though glowing enough to behold, must have been, on a fresh morning, pretty chilly to wear. He had evidently come out of his house in a hurry; and the priest was not surprised when he called out without further ceremony: "Did you hear that noise?"

"Yes," answered Father Brown. "I thought I had better look in, in case anything was the matter."

The Major looked at him rather queerly with his good-humoured gooseberry eyes. "What do you think the noise was?" he asked.

"It sounded like a gun or something," replied the other, with some hesitation; "but it seemed to have a singular sort of echo."

The Major was still looking at him quietly, but with protruding eyes, when the front door was flung open, releasing a flood of gaslight on the face of the fading mist; and another figure in pyjamas sprang or tumbled out into the garden. The figure was much longer, leaner, and more athletic; the pyjamas, though equally tropical, were comparatively taste-ful, being of white with a light lemon-yellow stripe. The man was haggard, but handsome, more sunburned than the other; he had an aquiline profile and rather deep-sunken eyes, and a slight air of oddity arising from the combination of coal-black hair with a much lighter moustache. All this Father Brown absorbed in detail more at leisure. For the moment he only saw one thing about the man: which was the revolver in his hand.

"Cray!" exclaimed the Major, staring at him, "did you fire that shot?"

"Yes, I did," retorted the black-haired gentleman hotly, "and so would you in my place. If you were chased everywhere by devils and nearly——"

The Major seemed to intervene rather hurriedly. "This is my friend Father Brown," he said. And then to Brown: "I don't know whether you've met Colonel Cray of the Royal Artillery."

"I have heard of him, of course," said the priest innocently. "Did you—did you hit anything?"

"I thought so," answered Cray with gravity.

"Did he——" asked Major Putnam, in a lowered voice, "did he fall or cry out, or anything?"

Colonel Cray was regarding his host with a strange and steady stare. "I'll tell you exactly what he did," he said. "He sneezed."

Father Brown's hand went half-way to his head, with the gesture of a man remembering somebody's name. He knew now what it was that was neither soda-water nor the snorting of a dog.

"Well," ejaculated the staring Major, "I never heard before that a service revolver was a thing to be sneezed at."

"Nor I," said Father Brown faintly. "It's lucky you didn't turn your artillery on him, or you might have given him quite a bad cold." Then, after a bewildered pause, he said: "Was it a burglar?"

"Let us go inside," said Major Putnam, rather sharply, and led the way into his house.

The interior exhibited a paradox often to be marked in such morning hours: that the rooms seemed brighter than the sky outside; even after the Major had turned out the one gaslight in the front hall. Father Brown was surprised to see the whole dining-table set out as for a festive meal, with napkins in their rings, and wine-glasses of some six unnecessary shapes set beside every plate. It was common enough, at that time of the morning, to find the remains of a banquet overnight; but to find it freshly spread so early was unusual.

While he stood wavering in the hall Major Putnam rushed past him and sent a raging eye over the whole oblong of the tablecloth. At last he spoke, spluttering: "All the silver gone!" he gasped. "Fish-knives and forks gone. Old cruet-stand gone. Even old silver cream-jug gone. And now, Father Brown, I am ready to answer your question of whether it was a burglar."

"They're simply a blind," said Cray stubbornly. "I know better than you why people persecute this house; I know better than you why——"

The Major patted him on the shoulder with a gesture almost peculiar to the soothing of a sick child, and said: "It was a burglar. Obviously it was a burglar."

"A burglar with a bad cold," observed Father Brown, "that might assist you to trace him in the neighbourhood."

The Major shook his head in a sombre manner. "He must be far beyond tracing now, I fear," he said.

Then, as the restless man with the revolver turned again towards the door into the garden, he added in a husky, confidential voice: "I doubt whether I should send for the police, for fear my friend here has been a little too free with his bullets, and got on the wrong side of the law. He's lived in very wild places; and, to be frank with you, I think he sometimes fancies things."

"I think you once told me," said Brown, "that he believes some Indian secret society is pursuing him."

Major Putnam nodded, but at the same time shrugged his shoulders. "I suppose we'd better follow him outside," he said. "I don't want any more—shall we say, sneezing?"

They passed out into the morning light, which was now even tinged with sunshine, and saw Colonel Cray's tall figure bent almost double, minutely examining the condition of gravel and grass. While the Major strolled unobtrusively towards him, the priest took an equally indolent turn, which took him round the next corner of the house to within a yard or two of the projecting dustbin.

He stood regarding this dismal object for some minute and a half; then he stepped towards it, lifted the lid, and put his head inside. Dust and other discolouring matter shook upwards as he did so; but Father Brown never observed his own appearance, whatever else he observed. He remained thus for a measurable period, as if engaged in some mysterious prayers. Then he came out again, with some ashes on his hair, and walked unconcernedly away.

By the time he came round to the garden door again he found a group there which seemed to roll away morbidities as the sunlight had already rolled away the mists. It was in no way rationally reassuring; it was simply broadly comic, like a cluster of Dickens's characters. Major Putnam had managed to slip inside and plunge into a proper shirt and trousers, with a crimson cummer-bund, and a light square jacket over all; thus normally set off, his red festive face seemed bursting with a commonplace cordiality. He was indeed emphatic, but then he was talking to his cook—the swarthy son of Malta, whose lean, yellow, and rather careworn face

contrasted quaintly with his snow-white cap and costume. The cook
might well be careworn, for cookery was the Major's hobby. He was one of
those amateurs who always know more than the professional. The only
other person he even admitted to be a judge of an omelette was his friend
Cray—and as Brown remembered this, he turned to look for the other
officer. In the new presence of daylight and people clothed and in their
right mind, the sight of him was rather a shock. The taller and more
elegant man was still in his night-garb, with tousled black hair, and now
crawling about the garden on his hands and knees, still looking for traces
of the burglar; and now and again, to all appearance, striking the ground
with his hand in anger at not finding him. Seeing him thus quadrupedal
in the grass, the priest raised his eyebrows rather sadly; and for the first
time guessed that "fancies things" might be an euphemism.

The third item in the group of the cook and the epicure was also known
to Father Brown: it was Audrey Watson, the Major's ward and housekeeper; and at this moment, to judge by her apron, tucked-up sleeves, and
resolute manner, much more the housekeeper than the ward.

"It serves you right," she was saying: "I always told you not to have that
old-fashioned cruet-stand."

"I prefer it," said Putnam placably. "I'm old-fashioned myself; and the
things keep together."

"And vanish together, as you see," she retorted. "Well, if you are not
going to bother about the burglar, I shouldn't bother about the lunch.
It's Sunday, and we can't send for vinegar and all that in the town; and
you Indian gentlemen can't enjoy what you call a dinner without a lot of
hot things. I wish to goodness now you hadn't asked Cousin Oliver to
take me to the musical service. It isn't over till half-past twelve, and the
Colonel has to leave by then. I don't believe you men can manage
alone."

"Oh, yes, we can, my dear," said the Major, looking at her very
amiably. "Marco has all the sauces; and we've often done ourselves well
in very rough places, as you might know by now. And it's time you had a
treat, Audrey; you mustn't be a housekeeper every hour of the day; and I
know you want to hear the music."

"I want to go to church," she said, with rather severe eyes.

She was one of those handsome women who will always be handsome,
because the beauty is not in an air or a tint, but in the very structure of the
head and features. But though she was not yet middle-aged and her
auburn hair was of a Titianesque fullness in form and colour, there was a
look in her mouth and around her eyes which suggested that some
sorrows wasted her, as winds waste at last the edges of a Greek temple. For
indeed the little domestic difficulty of which she was now speaking so

decisively was rather comic than tragic. Father Brown gathered, from the course of the conversation, that Cray, the other *gourmet*, had to leave before the usual lunch-time; but that Putnam, his host, not to be done out of a final feast with an old crony, had arranged for a special *déjeuner* to be set out and consumed in the course of the morning, while Audrey and other graver persons were at morning service. She was going there under the escort of a relative and old friend of hers, Dr. Oliver Oman, who, though a scientific man of a somewhat bitter type, was enthusiastic for music, and would go even to church to get it. There was nothing in all this that could conceivably concern the tragedy in Miss Watson's face; and by a half-conscious instinct, Father Brown turned again to the seeming lunatic grubbing about in the grass.

When he strolled across to him, the black unbrushed head was lifted abruptly, as if in some surprise at his continued presence. And indeed, Father Brown, for reasons best known to himself, had lingered much longer than politeness required; or even, in the ordinary sense, permitted.

"Well!" cried Cray, with wild eyes. "I suppose you think I'm mad, like the rest?"

"I have considered the thesis," answered the little man composedly. "And I incline to think you are not."

"What do you mean?" snapped Cray quite savagely.

"Real madmen," explained Father Brown, "always encourage their own morbidity. They never strive against it. But you are trying to find traces of the burglar; even when there aren't any. You are struggling against it. You want what no madman ever wants."

"And what is that?"

"You want to be proved wrong," said Brown.

During the last words, Cray had sprung or staggered to his feet and was regarding the cleric with agitated eyes. "By hell, but that is a true word!" he cried. "They are all at me here that the fellow was only after the silver—as if I shouldn't be only too pleased to think so! *She's* been at me," and he tossed his tousled black head towards Audrey, but the other had no need of the direction, "she's been at me to-day about how cruel I was to shoot a poor harmless housebreaker, and how I have the devil in me against poor harmless natives. But I was a good-natured man once—as good-natured as Putnam."

After a pause he said: "Look here, I've never seen you before; but you shall judge of the whole story: Old Putnam and I were friends in the same mess; but, owing to some accidents on the Afghan border, I got my regiment much sooner than most men; only we were both invalided home for a bit. I was engaged to Audrey out there; and we all travelled back together. But on the journey back things happened. Curious things. The result of them was that Putnam wants it broken off, and even Audrey keeps it hanging on—and I know what they mean. I know what they think I am. So do you.

"Well, these are the facts: The last day we were in an Indian city, I asked Putnam if I could get some Trichinopoli cigars; he directed me to a little place opposite his lodgings. I have since found he was quite right; but 'opposite' is a dangerous word when one decent house stands opposite five or six squalid ones: and I must have mistaken the door. It opened with difficulty, and then only on darkness; but as I turned back, the door behind me sank back and settled into its place with a noise as of innumerable bolts. There was nothing to do but to walk forward; which I did through passage after passage, pitch-dark. Then I came to a flight of steps, and then to a blind door, secured by a latch of elaborate Eastern iron-work, which I could only trace by touch, but which I loosened at last. I came out again upon gloom, which was half turned into a greenish twilight by a multitude of small but steady lamps below. They showed merely the feet or fringes of some huge and empty architecture. Just in front of me was something that looked like a mountain. I confess I nearly fell on the great stone platform on which I had emerged, to realise that it was an idol. And, worst of all, an idol with its back to me.

"It was hardly half human, I guessed; to judge by the small squat head, and still more by a thing like a tail or extra limb turned up behind and pointing, like a loathsome large finger, at some symbol graven in the centre of the vast stone back. I had begun, in the dim light, to guess at the hieroglyphic, not without horror, when a more horrible thing happened. A door opened silently in the temple wall behind me and a man came out, with a brown face and a black coat. He had a carved smile on his face, of copper flesh and ivory teeth; but I think the most hateful thing about him was that he was in European dress. I was prepared, I think, for shrouded priests or naked fakirs. But this seemed to say that the devilry was over all the earth. As indeed I found it to be.

" 'If you had only seen the Monkey's Feet,' he said, smiling steadily and without other preface, 'we should have been very gentle—you would only be tortured and die. If you had seen the Monkey's Face, still we should be very moderate, very tolerant—you would only be tortured and live. But as you have seen the Monkey's Tail, we must pronounce the worst sentence. Which is—Go Free.'

"When he said the words I heard the elaborate iron latch with which I had struggled automatically unlock itself: and then far down the dark passages I had passed I heard the heavy street-door shifting its own bolts backwards.

" 'It is vain to ask for mercy; you must go free,' said the smiling man. 'Henceforth a hair shall slay you like a sword, and a breath shall bite you like an adder; weapons shall come against you out of nowhere; and you shall die many times.' And with that he was swallowed once more in the wall behind; and I went out into the street."

Cray paused: and Father Brown unaffectedly sat down on the lawn and began to pick daisies.

Then the soldier continued: "Putnam, of course, with his jolly common sense, pooh-poohed all my fears; and from that time dates his doubt of my mental balance. Well, I'll simply tell you, in the fewest words, the three things that have happened since; and you shall judge which of us is right.

"The first happened in an Indian village on the edge of the jungle, but hundreds of miles from the temple, or town, or type of tribes and customs where the curse had been put on me. I woke in black midnight, and lay thinking of nothing in particular, when I felt a faint tickling thing, like a thread or a hair, trailed across my throat. I shrank back out of its way, and could not help thinking of the words in the temple. But when I got up and sought lights and a mirror, the line across my neck was a line of blood.

"The second happened in a lodging in Port Said, later, on our journey home together. It was a jumble of tavern and curiosity-shop; and though there was nothing there remotely suggesting the cult of the Monkey, it is, of course, possible that some of its images or talismans were in such a place. Its curse was there, anyhow. I woke again in the dark with a sensation that could not be put in colder or more literal words than that a breath bit like an adder. Existence was an agony of extinction; I dashed my head against walls until I dashed it against a window; and fell rather than jumped into the garden below. Putnam, poor fellow, who had called the other thing a chance scratch, was bound to take seriously the fact of finding me half insensible on the grass at dawn. But I fear it was my mental state he took seriously; and not my story.

"The third happened in Malta. We were in a fortress there; and as it happened our bedrooms overlooked the open sea, which almost came up to our window-sills, save for a flat white outer wall as bare as the sea. I woke up again; but it was not dark. There was a full moon, as I walked to the window; I could have seen a bird on the bare battlement, or a sail on the horizon. What I did see was a sort of stick or branch circling self-supported in the empty sky. It flew straight in at my window and smashed the lamp beside the pillow I had just quitted. It was one of those queer-shaped war-clubs some Eastern tribes use. But it had come from no human hand."

Father Brown threw away a daisy chain he was making, and rose with a wistful look. "Has Major Putnam," he asked, "got any Eastern curios, idols, weapons, and so on, from which one might get a hint?"

"Plenty of those, though not much use, I fear," replied Cray; "but by all means come into his study."

As they entered they passed Miss Watson buttoning her gloves for church, and heard the voice of Putnam downstairs still giving a lecture on cookery to the cook. In the Major's study and den of curios they came suddenly on a third party, silk-hatted and dressed for the street, who was poring over an open book on the smoking-table—a book which he dropped rather guiltily, and turned.

Cray introduced him civilly enough, as Dr. Oman, but he showed such disfavour in his very face that Brown guessed the two men, whether Audrey knew it or not, were rivals. Nor was the priest wholly unsympathetic with the prejudice. Dr. Oman was a very well-dressed gentleman indeed; well-featured, though almost dark enough for an Asiatic. But Father Brown had to tell himself sharply that one should be in charity even with those who wax their pointed beards, who have small gloved hands, and who speak with perfectly modulated voices.

Cray seemed to find something specially irritating in the small prayer-book in Oman's dark-gloved hand. "I didn't know that was in your line," he said rather rudely.

Oman laughed mildly, but without offence. "This is more so, I know," he said, laying his hand on the big book he had dropped, "a dictionary of drugs and such things. But it's rather too large to take to church." Then he closed the larger book, and there seemed again the faintest touch of hurry and embarrassment.

"I suppose," said the priest, who seemed anxious to change the subject, "all these spears and things are from India?"

"From everywhere," answered the doctor. "Putnam is an old soldier, and has been in Mexico and Australia, and the Cannibal Islands for all I know."

"I hope it was not in the Cannibal Islands," said Brown, "that he learnt the art of cookery." And he ran his eye over the stew-pots or other strange utensils on the wall.

At this moment the jolly subject of their conversation thrust his laughing, lobsterish face into the room. "Come along, Cray," he cried. "Your lunch is just coming in. And the bells are ringing for those who want to go to church."

Cray slipped upstairs to change; Dr. Oman and Miss Watson betook themselves solemnly down the street, with a string of other churchgoers; but Father Brown noticed that the doctor twice looked back and scrutinised the house; and even came back to the corner of the street to look at it again.

The priest looked puzzled. "*He* can't have been at the dustbin," he muttered. "Not in those clothes. Or was he here earlier to-day?"

Father Brown, touching other people, was as sensitive as a barometer; but to-day he seemed about as sensitive as a rhinoceros. By no social law, rigid or implied, could he be supposed to linger round the lunch of the Anglo-Indian friends; but he lingered, covering his position with torrents of amusing but quite needless conversation. He was the more puzzling because he did not seem to want any lunch. As one after another of the most exquisitely balanced kedgerees or curries, accompanied with their appropriate vintages, were laid before the other two, he only repeated that it was one of his fast-days, and munched a piece of bread and sipped and then left untasted a tumbler of cold water. His talk, however, was exuberant.

"I'll tell you what I'll do for you," he cried; "I'll mix you a salad! I can't eat it, but I'll mix it like an angel! You've got a lettuce there."

"Unfortunately it's the only thing we have got," answered the good-humoured Major. "You must remember that mustard, vinegar, oil, and so on vanished with the cruet and the burglar."

"I know," replied Brown, rather vaguely. "That's what I've always been afraid would happen. That's why I always carry a cruet-stand about with me. I'm so fond of salads."

And to the amazement of the two men he took a pepper-pot out of his waistcoat pocket and put it on the table.

"I wonder why the burglar wanted mustard, too," he went on, taking a mustard-pot from another pocket. "A mustard plaster, I suppose. And vinegar," producing that condiment, "haven't I heard something about vinegar and brown paper? As for oil, which I think I put in my left——"

His garrulity was an instant arrested; for lifting his eyes, he saw what no one else saw—the black figure of Dr. Oman standing on the sunlit lawn and looking steadily into the room. Before he could quite recover himself, Cray had cloven in.

"You're an astounding card," he said, staring. "I shall come and hear your sermons if they're as amusing as your manners." His voice changed a little, and he leaned back in his chair.

"Oh, there are sermons in a cruet-stand, too," said Father Brown, quite gravely. "Have you heard of faith like a grain of mustard-seed; or charity that anoints with oil? And as for vinegar, can any soldiers forget that solitary soldier, who, when the sun was darkened——"

Colonel Cray leaned forward a little and clutched the tablecloth.

Father Brown, who was making the salad, tipped two spoonfuls of the mustard into the tumbler of water beside him; stood up, and said in a new, loud and sudden voice—"Drink that!"

At the same moment the motionless doctor in the garden came running and bursting open a window, cried, "Am I wanted? Has he been poisoned?"

"Pretty near," said Brown, with the shadow of a smile; for the emetic had very suddenly taken effect. And Cray lay in a deck-chair, gasping as for life, but alive.

Major Putnam had sprung up, his purple face mottled. "A crime!" he cried hoarsely. "I will go for the police!"

The priest could hear him dragging down his palm-leaf hat from the peg and tumbling out of the front door; he heard the garden gate slam. But he only stood looking at Cray; and after a silence said quietly:

"I shall not talk to you much; but I will tell you what you want to know. There is no curse on you. The Temple of the Monkey was either a coincidence or a part of the trick; the trick was the trick of a white man. There is only one weapon that will bring blood with that mere feathery touch: a razor held by a white man. There is one way of making a common room full of invisible overpowering poison: turning on the gas—the crime of a white man. And there is only one kind of club that can be thrown out of a window, turn in mid air and come back to the window next to it: the Australian boomerang. You'll see some of them in the Major's study."

With that he went outside and spoke for a moment to the doctor. The moment after, Audrey Watson came rushing into the house and fell on her knees beside Cray's chair. He could not hear what they said to each other; but their faces moved with amazement, not unhappiness. The doctor and the priest walked slowly towards the garden gate.

"I suppose the Major was in love with her, too," he said, with a sigh; and when the other nodded observed: "You were very generous, doctor. You did a fine thing. But what made you suspect?"

"A very small thing," said Oman; "but it kept me restless in church till I came back to see that all was well. That book on his table was a work on poisons; and was put down open at the place where it stated that a certain Indian poison, though deadly and difficult to trace, was particularly easily reversible by the use of the commonest emetics. I suppose he read that at the last moment——"

"And remembered that there were emetics in the cruet-stand," said Father Brown. "Exactly. He threw the cruet in the dustbin, where I found it, along with other silver, for the sake of a burglary blind. But if you look at that pepper-pot I put on the table, you'll see a small hole. That's where

Cray's bullet struck, shaking up the pepper and making the criminal sneeze."

There was a silence. Then Dr. Oman said grimly: "The Major is a long time looking for the police."

"Or the police in looking for the Major?" said the priest. "Well, goodbye."

DOVER · THRIFT · EDITIONS

All books complete and unabridged. All 5³⁄₁₆″ × 8¹⁄₄″, paperbound.
Just $1.00 each in U.S.A.

FICTION

FLATLAND: A ROMANCE OF MANY DIMENSIONS, Edwin A. Abbott. 96pp. 27263-X

BEOWULF, Beowulf (trans. by R. K. Gordon). 64pp. 27264-8

ALICE'S ADVENTURES IN WONDERLAND, Lewis Carroll. 80pp. 27543-4

FIVE GREAT SHORT STORIES, Anton Chekhov. 96pp. 26463-7

FAVORITE FATHER BROWN STORIES, G. K. Chesterton. 96pp. 27545-0

HEART OF DARKNESS, Joseph Conrad. 80pp. 26464-5

THE SECRET SHARER AND OTHER STORIES, Joseph Conrad. 128pp. 27546-9

THE OPEN BOAT AND OTHER STORIES, Stephen Crane. 112pp. 27547-7

THE RED BADGE OF COURAGE, Stephen Crane. 112pp. 26465-3

A CHRISTMAS CAROL, Charles Dickens. 80pp. 26865-9

NOTES FROM THE UNDERGROUND, Fyodor Dostoyevsky. 96pp. 27053-X

SIX GREAT SHERLOCK HOLMES STORIES, Sir Arthur Conan Doyle. 112pp. 27055-6

THE OVERCOAT AND OTHER SHORT STORIES, Nikolai Gogol. 112pp. 27057-2

GREAT GHOST STORIES, John Grafton (ed.). 112pp. 27270-2

THE LUCK OF ROARING CAMP AND OTHER SHORT STORIES, Bret Harte. 96pp. 27271-0

YOUNG GOODMAN BROWN AND OTHER SHORT STORIES, Nathaniel Hawthorne. 128pp. 27060-2

THE GIFT OF THE MAGI AND OTHER SHORT STORIES, O. Henry. 96pp. 27061-0

THE BEAST IN THE JUNGLE AND OTHER STORIES, Henry James. 128pp. 27552-3

THE TURN OF THE SCREW, Henry James. 96pp. 26684-2

DUBLINERS, James Joyce. 160pp. 26870-5

THE CALL OF THE WILD, Jack London. 64pp. 26472-6

FIVE GREAT SHORT STORIES, Jack London. 96pp. 27063-7

WHITE FANG, Jack London. 160pp. 26968-X

THE NECKLACE AND OTHER SHORT STORIES, Guy de Maupassant. 128pp. 27064-5

BARTLEBY AND BENITO CERENO, Herman Melville. 112pp. 26473-4

THE GOLD-BUG AND OTHER TALES, Edgar Allan Poe. 128pp. 26875-6

THE STRANGE CASE OF DR. JEKYLL AND MR. HYDE, Robert Louis Stevenson. 64pp. 26688-5

TREASURE ISLAND, Robert Louis Stevenson. 160pp. 27559-0

THE MYSTERIOUS STRANGER AND OTHER STORIES, Mark Twain. 128pp. 27069-6

CANDIDE, Voltaire (François-Marie Arouet). 112pp. 26689-3

THE INVISIBLE MAN, H. G. Wells. 112pp. (Available in U.S. only.) 27071-8

ETHAN FROME, Edith Wharton. 96pp. 26690-7